Fifty Shades of Pink

AN LA LOVERS NOVELLA

JOURDYN KELLY

Also by Jourdyn Kelly

Fifty Shades of Pink

The Club

THE THINGS YOU do for friends. Miranda, my best friend who doesn't look happy with me at all at the moment, glares at me. Shit. Did I really say that out loud?

"Cassidy, if you're going to grumble all night, you can leave." She stares at me, her fiery red hair a perfect complement to her being pissed at me right now.

"Sorry," I mumble. She knows I hate it when she calls me Cassidy. It's Cass, damn it. But it's her night. I have to be the supportive best friend, do what she wants to do, and be happy about it. I can be unselfish for the next couple of hours. I think. Though why she chose to come to an uppity place like this for her bachelorette party, I'll never understand.

Miranda and I have been friends since we were in grade school. Now, at twenty-five, she decides she's ready to get married. Personally I think she's too young. We're the same age, and there's no way in hell *I'm* ready for marriage. Don't get me wrong, Connor is a great guy and all, but… well… he's taking my best friend away from me. Damn. I'm being selfish again.

I push past those depressing thoughts, and take in my surroundings. I should be grateful that we didn't go to some male strip club. I'm Miranda's 'token gay friend' as some of her other, not so nice friends call me. Fuck them. I've been in Miranda's life way longer than they have. So they're the 'token straight friends'. Of course, I don't say this to Rand. She has a hard enough time with having to defend me as it is. I just don't fit in with her group anymore. She gets pissed when I say that, but it's true. They're all girly girls. And then there's me.

I'm what they call androgynous. I'm taller than most girls, and because I was so lanky and awkward in high school, I began working out. Now my tall, lean body is muscular. Rand's other friends pretend they're not interested, but I've seen the way they look at me. Not to be conceited or anything, but I look damn good. My facial features are a little more feminine than most people would expect when they notice my body first (yes, I wear makeup. There's nothing wrong with that).

My dark hair is cut short in the back, but left long in the front. That was Rand's suggestion. My eyes are what Rand says give me "the advantage". Whatever that means. One is a light amber color that tends to "glow" in the sun, and darken when I'm… well, being passionate. The other is a shade of blue that most people think is unnatural. My point is, it's never a struggle for me to find female companionship if I want it. Even within Rand's little "straight" circle.

Not that I'll find anything I want here. I take in my surroundings as I wait for Rand to check in. Posh enough place. A bunch of leather in different colors. White, black, red. Lace in the same shades. I don't even know what the name of the place is, it's that exclusive. Not sure how Rand got in here. I mean, I know all of her friends. None of them are important enough to get an invite to what I'm told is the "most exclusive club around".

I turn to see if Rand was done, and something catches my eye (the blue one), and I stand there with what I'm sure is a look of stupid shock. Holy shit. This is bullshit! Rand told me this was some frou-frou club, but not *this* kind of club!

Rand smiles at the bouncer dude, and turns towards me with a huge smile on her face. It falters when she sees my expression, which I'm pretty positive is still stupid shock. I grab her arm, a little more roughly than I intend—how appropriate—and drag her away from the others.

"What the fuck, Rand?"

"Now, Cass, just calm down."

Oh sure. *Now* she calls me Cass. Because she knows I'm rightly pissed.

"Calm down? Why didn't you tell me this was a BDSM club?"

"I thought you knew." Her face is the picture of innocence. If I didn't know her better, I'd say she was telling the truth. But I do know her better.

"How would I know? I don't even know the *name* of this… this *place*! You know I'm not into this shit!"

Rand rolls her eyes. *Rolls her eyes! At me!* Not the greatest move there, oh best friend of mine.

"You know, I never thought you'd be so uptight. With as much sex as you have, and all the noises I've heard coming from your room, I thought you'd be more open-minded."

"I *am* open-minded," I hiss through clenched teeth. "But, I don't get this pain shit. Or *submitting* to some asswipe who thinks they own you."

Again with the eye roll.

"That's not at all what it's about," Rand tells me with an air of haughtiness. "You, of all people, should know not to judge what you don't understand."

"Oh? And *you* understand it?" It's my turn to roll my eyes. The Rand I know is as vanilla as it can get. Like, seriously. She even eats vanilla ice cream.

"Connor and I are very practiced in this lifestyle."

She says it so quietly I almost don't hear her. Once I figure out what that really means, it takes all of my willpower not to say "eww". I *think* it, but I don't say it. I do *not* need to know that about Rand's and Connor's sex life.

"That's… I don't even know what to say about that."

"Why should you say anything? It's really none of your business."

"Is that how you got an invitation here?" I ask, suddenly very curious as to how *into* this lifestyle Rand is.

"Connor and I are members."

My eyes bug out. She could have told me she had testicles, and I would have found that less shocking than what she just said.

"How did I not know this?"

"You don't know because I know how you feel about this. But you are my best friend. I wanted you to be here with me tonight. This is our last night out as single ladies. Let's have some fun!"

"Do they know?" I jerk my head towards the glam squad who were giggling and pointing. Mature.

"No. And I don't want them to. They think I got the invitation from someone at work."

"Why didn't you bring Connor? Don't you think you'd have more fun with him?"

Rand shakes her red curls at me. "Tonight is a free pass."

"Excuse me?" Why did I ask? I'm not going to like the answer. I know I'm not.

"We have tonight to do whatever we want with whomever we want." Her brown eyes flick away from me.

I *knew* I wasn't going to like her answer! Not only does she know I don't like this BDSM shit, but I abhor cheating! It's why I don't get into any damn relationships anymore. I've been cheated on too many times, and it hurts like a motherfucker.

"You're kidding me!"

"Cass." She pulls me closer. "I don't expect you to understand mine and Connor's relationship. But I do expect you to respect it."

"So you want me to sit around in this *place* while you go off and fuck some other dude?"

"I want you to get rid of your judgements, and try to have fun. Don't worry about what I'm doing, or who I'm doing it with." She engulfs me in a quick hug. "What you think of me matters to me, but I won't change for you. I've never asked that of you. Will you do the same for me?"

Well, shit. She had me there. When others bullied me for being gay or androgynous, Rand was always there to support me. Never once did she complain, judge or ask me to change. If this is what she likes, and Connor doesn't have a problem with it, who am I to say anything?

"Fine. Have fun doing your thing. I'll be at the bar, not judging. Just drinking."

Rand laughs. "No bar. We have a VIP section. The others are going to mingle. You should, too."

A large man in black leather, and a mask that hid more than half his face, touches Rand on the shoulder. She smiles at him before turning back to me.

"I have to go. Please, Cass. Have some fun. It's not as bad as you think."

5

The Invitation

NOT AS BAD as I think. I doubt that. I sit back in the plush leather couch—alone—and people watch. Can't say it's not entertaining. I notice that there are an equal number of women who are dominating as there are men. Dominatrixes? Is that what they're called? Hell, I'll admit I know nothing about this lifestyle. What's interesting is there are women going off with Dominatrixes. Seems a little counterproductive to me. We all want to be strong, right? So why would we submit to another woman? Sure, it's sexy as shit, definitely more so than seeing a woman go off with a dominating man.

It makes me wonder. Wonder what I would do if I was with someone who wanted to dominate me. I think about that for a moment, and shake my head slightly. Nope. Never happen. I just can't imagine being turned on by someone wanting to hurt me, or control me. Then I turned it around in my head. Could I control someone? Hurt them? Again, I shake my head. Nope. I can't see being turned on by someone being in pain because of me.

Even so, this place? It's intriguing. Not raunchy, but classy, despite the leather. High-end liquors—I take a sip of the single malt scotch I had ordered, and savor it. High-end people. Oh god! What if they do drugs here? What if Rand is doing drugs? I shake that off, too. She would never...

"I didn't order this," I call to the waitress that interrupted my inner musings by placing a shot glass of amber liquid in front of me.

"It's from Mistress," the young woman answers. Her voice holds a bit of awe when she says Mistress, and I'm immediately interested in what or who could cause that reaction. I look behind me, then to each side, but I see no one who is focused on me. I raise the shot glass in the air, a salute to whomever may or may not be watching, and slam it back. Holy fuck that stings! Fireball whiskey. My eyes water, but I will myself not to cough or show any kind of outward discomfort. Though in a place like this I'm sure my discomfort will turn my admirer on.

I glance at my watch. We've been here for thirty minutes, and I haven't seen Rand or the others since we came in. I try not to think about that. Instead, I wonder if I'm going to get another shot. Or maybe an invitation. I'd have to turn it down, but it's always nice to know you're wanted. With that thought running through my mind, I almost miss the light pink fingernails that tap a pink card laying upon my table. Funny, I didn't notice that there before.

I bring my eyes up in time to see the most perfect, white leather clad ass I have ever seen in my entire life. Seriously, if I were a man, that ass would have me at full attention in less than 30 seconds. As it is, everything that I have that *can* stand at attention, is. Somehow I tear my eyes away from the sway of perfection, and pick up the pink card. Turning it over to examine it, I realize there's nothing on it at all. It's completely blank. Just a plain, pink card.

"Excuse me," I call out, flagging down the waitress that gave me the shot. She smiles at me, then sees the card in my hand. I swear, if her eyes got any bigger, they'd probably pop out of her head. "What is this?"

"Where did you get that?" Well, hell. Why did she have to sound all accusatory? I'm just sitting here minding my own damn business.

"Some woman left it on my table, then walked that way." I point towards a darkened hallway.

"*She* left this?"

Again with the awe. "Who is *she*?"

"Mistress." The young waitress shakes her head. "I always thought this was a myth." Her mouth snaps shut, and she looks around. I look around with her, and wonder what the deal is. It's not like she gave up the secret of life. Shit, she hasn't even really told me what this damn card means. Myth?

"Mind telling me what the 'myth' means?" I ask, trying not to sound as frustrated as I am.

"She wants you."

"Who?"

"Mistress."

Is this "Mistress" the one with the perfect ass? Because if so, I'm seriously reconsidering my position on BDSM. Great. Now I'm thinking about positions with Mistress.

"What do I do with this?" I wave the card in front of her still bugging eyes.

She looks around again. What? She doesn't know?

"You're to go to the Pink Room." She looks at me now. *Really* looks at me. Hey, it's fine. I know I look good tonight. I'm wearing black boots and jeans with a crisp, white button-up shirt. It was unbuttoned enough that if I had cleavage, it would be showing. The sleeves were rolled up to the elbows revealing some of my tattoos. I don't have full sleeve tattoos, just a few really important ones on my arms and chest. Okay, maybe a few in a few other strategic places.

"And where would that be?" I ask after giving her a full minute to peruse my body. I don't know if she's impressed or not. Frankly, I don't care. I just want to know who this Mistress is, and what she wants from me.

"Follow me."

The Meeting

WHAT AM I getting myself into? Why am I even following this chick to this "pink room" at the behest of some 'mistress' I haven't even seen? Okay, I've seen her ass. And that alone was reason enough, apparently, to get my ass up and walking down this darkened hall.

The 'waitress-in-awe' stops in front of a soft pink door, the same shade of the nails I saw tapping the card.

"In here," she says, glancing once at the door (is that jealousy in her eyes?) before hurrying away.

Now what? Do I knock? Just go in? I decide to tap lightly on the door. When I don't hear anything, I let myself in. My breath catches in my throat, my mouth is dry (other parts, not so much), and I'm not sure I have a coherent thought in my mind other than I want her under me. And, all of that happens without seeing her face. That's right. She has a mask on. Much like the one the dude that took Rand away had on, only Mistress's was white to match her outfit.

"Come."

Oh, honey. With a body like that, and a voice as sweet as yours, I could definitely come. *If* I had use of my tongue *that's* what I would have said. Or I would be using my tongue for something much more pleasurable than talking. Unfortunately, nothing was working. Not my tongue, not my brain, not even my legs. So I just stand there. Like an idiot. She's probably thinking she just made a huge mistake picking me out of the lot.

"Sit."

Her eyes flicker to the chair that is directly in front of her. *She* sits with impeccable posture, her hands clasped together on her lap. Her ankles were crossed in an almost relaxed state, but I can see tension. Maybe I was imagining that. What could she possibly have to be tense about. *I* was the one being ordered around like a dog.

She tilts her head to the side, her exquisite silver—that's the only way I know how to describe them—eyes never leave mine. Her long, golden locks fall over her shoulder as she studies me.

"You don't like being told what to do."

It's not a question, so I don't bother answering. I probably couldn't anyway. You know, my tongue being all tied and shit. I still don't move, but she does. She begins to rise, and suddenly my tongue and feet decide to work again.

"Wait!" I quickly move to the chair, and sit. Look, I may not understand this BDSM shit, but I'm not a damn fool. This woman is gorgeous—what I can see of her. I'm not about to miss an opportunity to be with her. Besides, who says I can't turn the tables once we've started?

"Why are you here?"

Goddamn, but her voice makes me tingle all over. I want to give her everything she wants. Answers, orgasms, kids. Fuck, I don't care what she wants, I just want to give it to her. She must be really good at what she does. And that thought sobers me pretty quickly. I just learned that I do *not* like thinking about her with others.

"I'm here in support of my friend." A friend who practically abandoned me the moment we got here. To fuck some stranger before she got married. "Of course I haven't seen her since."

She nods. "Miranda. She and her friends are being well taken care of. You didn't join in the fun."

"Not my scene." I don't like the bitter taste in my mouth thinking about Rand and what she was doing.

"You don't approve."

I shrug. Again, it wasn't a question. "Who am I to judge? I'm sure you get a lot of cheaters in here. Part of the reason I could never get into this lifestyle. What if I did something wrong? Forgot to obey? My '*Dom*' would just find someone who would, right?" Yeah, yeah. I'm judging again. I can't help it. I have no reason to feel this insane jealousy when it comes to the woman in front of me. I don't even know her name. But it hurt more thinking about her being with others the way Rand was than it did when I was cheated on by those I thought I cared about. Irrational.

"You have no idea what this lifestyle is about, do you?" I shake my head. There's no need in denying it. "Would it make you feel better if I told you that Connor is with Miranda?"

I frown in confusion. That's definitely not what Rand told me she was going to do.

"They don't know it's each other," she continues as if reading my mind. "They wanted a different experience, so we're giving them one. They'll see that all they really need is each other at the end of the night.

The purpose of this place is not to tear people apart, Cassidy. It's to bring fire to the relationship. To give them something more than what they have right now. It's not for everyone. But for those who enjoy it, it does not make them bad people."

My mind began reeling the moment I heard her say my name.

"How did you know my name?"

She gives me a small smile. "This is my club. I make it my business to know what goes on in here. Do you feel better about Miranda now?"

I shrug again. She still wanted to sleep with someone else. And now I have this vision of Rand and Connor doing... this.

"Would you like to learn more about what we do here, Cassidy?"

She tilts her head again when I don't answer. I don't know what it is about that small gesture, but it makes my stomach clench. I find it sexy. There's just something vulnerable in the action that doesn't fit her confident aura. She begins to rise again, and again I find myself scrambling to keep her there.

"Yes." Damn. Was that my voice? Since when does it tremble?

There is no smile, no look of relief in her eyes, but they do flash with desire. That much I do know. I've seen that look many times in a woman's eyes. Never one quite as captivating as the woman in front of me.

"Let me bind your hands."

My eyes leave her luscious cleavage at the demand. "Take off your mask," I counter.

"No. If you can't comply, Cassidy, we're wasting our time here."

"You mean submit?" She was going to leave again. I catch the dulling of her eyes. I need to get her to stay, and excited again. "I admit that I don't know much about this... stuff. But I'm pretty sure that trust is a big thing, right? Don't I need to trust whoever is going to be causing me pain?" My body shivers at the thought of the pain. I don't want to think of her getting off on my suffering.

"I don't want to cause you pain, Cassidy."

"Cass. Remove the mask. Please?"

"Since this is your first time, I'll compromise with you." She looks away, almost as though she was shocked by what she just said. When her eyes come back to mine, I see nothing but confidence. "Let me bind you, and I will take off the mask."

"Take the mask off first." Yeah, I know. I'm a defiant little shit. I don't like being told what to do. I've always been that way.

"You don't like authority." Another accurate statement from her. I wonder if I should be freaked out that she seems to know more about me than I know about her. Which is nothing. "If you want to learn, Cassidy," she emphasizes my name, "you're going to have to knock that chip off your shoulder. Or I can do it for you."

Yes, please. Do whatever you want to me. Okay, so I think I've just made my decision. Slowly, I put my hands behind my back. Another flash of her eyes, and she stands to walk behind me. I don't know where she got the silk to wrap around my hands, but in my mind it came from that beautiful, tanned cleavage.

"That wasn't so hard now, was it?" She breathes close to my ear. Good lord. My body reacts so intensely to this woman. I've never responded to *anyone* like this before. I turn my head hoping to be able to feel her lips on mine. Unfortunately, she moves away quickly. Damn it. She reassumes her stiff position in front of me.

"Now the mask." Oh yeah, I'm turned on. My voice always seems to lower an octave when I'm particularly horny. I think it just lowered two or more octaves for her.

True to her proposed compromise, she lifts her beautiful hair in the back, and brings forth a long ribbon. Holding the mask to her face with her left hand, she gently pulls the ribbon to untie it. Her eyes close briefly, making me wonder if she was regretting her decision. For a moment, I don't think she will go through with it. Then, with both hands she lowers the mask away from her face.

That gasp came from me. I know it did. If I thought her ass was the most perfect I've ever seen, it was *nothing* compared to the exquisiteness of her face. I could sit here and tell you every little detail like how perfect her nose was, or how full her lips were, but I'm too mesmerized.

"Are you ready for your next lesson?"

I wonder if I'm drooling. It's entirely possible that I am. That body, that face, that voice. This woman was *everyone's* wet dream all rolled into one delicious package. I've completely passed the point where I could deny her anything. But I'm not so far gone that I can't ask for something in return.

"What is your name?" Hey. It's worth a try.

"You may call me Mistress."

"You know my name." Wow. That sounded perilously like a whine. What the hell is this woman doing to me? Oh yeah. Anything she wants.

"I've given you the mask, Cassidy. That is all I'm willing to give you. Stand."

I don't hesitate this time, and am rewarded with a soft smile as she stands with me. It's not surprising that I'm taller than she is by a few inches. She seems so delicate. I think I'm about to be proven absolutely wrong about that.

"Walk to the edge of the bed."

There's a bed in here? Well, hell! Shows where my attention has been since entering this room. I glance over her shoulder. Hot damn. There it is. On rubbery legs, I obey. I feel the heat of her behind me, but I don't turn back around. I decide instead that I will wait for my next instructions. I know. Surprises me, too.

"Face me, Cassidy."

I think I've learned enough in the short amount of time we've been together not to correct her usage of my name. Oddly enough, I kind of like hearing my full name coming out of her mouth. Damn, that mouth. I want to feel it. Taste it. Enough to make me lean forward, only to be stopped by a firm hand on my chest.

"No touching. Not with your hands, not with your mouth." I manage to bite back the frustrated groan. Barely. She begins to unbutton my shirt, and I tremble with anticipation. "What's your favorite word, Cassidy?"

The question confuses me. My mind is certainly not functioning enough to make silly conversation. When her hands stop what they were doing, I look up (yes, you caught me. I was looking at her cleavage again). Shit. She's serious with this question?

"Um. Platypus."

She laughs softly. A magical sound. "Platypus?" I nod my head. It is! It's fun as shit to say. "All right then. That is your safe word. Should be easy for you to remember. If I do anything that you're not comfortable with, or you want me to stop, all you have to say is your safe word. I will stop without hesitation. Without question. Understand?"

I nod again. She smells so good. What is that? Lavender? Have I ever noticed how a woman smelled before? Well other than in obvious places? I don't think I've paid that much attention. All of my blood migrates south, leaving me light-headed, when she wraps her arms around me. Sadly, it's short lived as she just wanted to untether my hands. Oh how my hands itch to touch her.

"Remove your shirt." It keeps my hands busy, at least. She watches my movements with interest, eyes flickering with surprise when she realizes I'm not wearing a bra. Never do. My tits are small enough, and firm enough, not to warrant one. Judging by her reaction, I see she approves. Oh yeah, baby. I'm full of surprises.

Not only was my lack of a bra approved of, but she also seems quite captivated by my abs. Six pack, baby. I worked hard for this body. If a woman like Mistress is aroused by that, it was worth all of the time and pain. My muscles contract involuntarily when she feathers her fingers down my stomach.

The look of pure lust in her eyes nearly makes me come right then and there. She never says a word, or makes a sound, but those eyes. Man, they are so expressive it's like I can read them as clearly as any book I've ever read. Any *erotica* book.

"Unbutton your jeans, but leave them on." I readily do as she asks, itching to just take them off completely, and stand in front of this woman in all my glory. "Now get on the bed. Lay down in the middle, with your hands above your head."

I hop up on the bed, scooting my ass to the middle. Glancing behind me, I notice the bars that make up the headboard. Around a couple of the bars are ropes, and instead of making me nervous, the sight of them excites me. I lay down, extending my hands above my head, and wait.

"Grab ahold of this bar," she instructs. Once I do, she ties the rope around my wrist with a bit of strength. It's tight, biting into me, but not uncomfortable enough for me to complain. She walks around the bed, completing the task with my other hand, and then stands at the foot of the bed, letting her eyes roam my half-clad body. Come on, baby. Take of the jeans. You won't be sorry.

I wonder again if she can read my mind as she bends over slightly, hooking her fingers into the waistband of my jeans and boxer briefs.

"Lift."

I plant my feet flat on the bed, boots and all, and lift my hips. I grin when she hits a snag in getting my jeans off. The grin became a full-on arrogant smirk when she gasps at what she sees. When she looks at me, an elegant brow raises at my smirk, but she says nothing. She just licks her lips, then proceeds to divest me of my jeans and boots until I lay in front of her as naked as the day I was born. Except the tattoos, of course.

"Spread your legs."

Fuck. I can feel my excitement trickling down the crack of my ass, making me squirm a little.

"More, Cassidy!"

I look from her to the bedposts and back again. She wants me to spread myself open that far? Was humility a part of the lifestyle? I've never bared myself that much to *anyone*. She remains quiet, waiting, tapping that pale pink nail against the wood of the post. She's losing patience with me again. Taking a deep breath, I spread myself for her until she was able to reach the ropes around my ankles.

"Good girl." She pats the side of my calf, and walks away. My gaze tracks her to an armoire that stands a few feet from the bed. Geez. I *really* didn't notice anything in this room except her. It's pink! The bed, the walls, all pink. Not ugly, Pepto pink, but a subtle, almost calming color. Like her nails. Huh. I guess that's why they call it the Pink Room.

My eyes bulge when I see what's nestled in that armoire. Fuck. How can such a girly, pretty room be equipped for such torture? Warily, I watch her run her finger over a few of her instruments, coming to a stop on what looks like a leather fringed... whip. Shit.

After making her selection, she closes the armoire, and makes her way back to me. Snapping the whip across her palm the entire time. My body seems to jump involuntarily with each sound of the leather against her flesh. She stands beside me, tickling the fringe down my ribcage. With a flick of her wrist the leather slaps me smartly on my side. I let out a hiss as the sting moves through my body.

"Do you always wear that?" She asks, nodding to the dildo that's buried inside me on one end, and standing proudly at attention on the other. I nod, and she slaps the whip across my nipple. Shit that hurts! "Answer me!"

"Yes." Another slap, another hiss, and perhaps a bit of movement of my body trying to get away from her.

"Yes, what?"

Okay, *this* I have a problem with. I don't want to fucking call her Mistress. I want to know her name! I highly doubt I could get away with calling her baby or snookums. Sigh.

"Yes, Mistress."

"And, do you use it often?" I shrug. Big mistake! I receive two stinging slaps for that one. "Tell me the truth, Cassidy."

"I used to, Mistress. Not so much these days." Shit. I really *did* tell her the truth. So much for being all mysterious and shit. She has that covered well enough, I suppose.

"Why?"

Not wanting to get hit again, I immediately open my mouth, and the truth just comes tumbling out.

"I haven't found anyone that holds my interest lately, Mistress." Whew! That was a late 'mistress', and I rush to slip it in there before she can punish me for it.

"Do I hold your interest, Cassidy?"

I look her in the eyes, hoping to convey the absolute truth to her beyond my words. "Yes, Mistress. Very much so."

She gives me a 'reward' by fanning the fringe lightly across both of my tits. I have to admit it feels good enough that I almost loosen my grip on the headboard. Her eyes travel to my hands, which I'm sure if I look at them I'll see white knuckles. My whole body is tense.

She leans closer, brushing her fingertips over my cheek, down my neck, and down the length of my torso. She stops before touching my little helper. Damn it.

"I don't want to hurt you, Cassidy. That's not what this is about." Her hand moves up my arm until her fingers tap my strong grip. "Relax.

Loosen your grip. Your brain is anticipating the pain, your body bracing for it. So much so that you can't feel the pleasure that being like this can give you."

"Easy for you to say." Yes, I'm a dumbass and said that right out loud. "Why don't you lay here all tied up, and let me hit you. See if *you* like it." Yep. Said that, too. I'm an idiot.

She frowns. "Say your safe word, Cassidy."

I don't want to. As much as it hurts, I don't want it to end, so I clamp my traitorous mouth shut.

"I know what it's like to be hit. The kind of hitting that *doesn't* come with pleasure at the end of it." There's that surprise in her features again. She didn't mean to say that. Of course, I nearly miss her surprise because of the rage that fills me. Who would dare hurt this beautiful creature?

"I'll kill them!" Oh shit. I said *that* out loud, too. I *really* need to get this mouth under control. I'm almost afraid to look at her. Afraid that I have ruined everything by being too personal. She doesn't give me a choice when her fingertips guide my chin until I'm drowning in her gaze.

"You're sweet." I blush. What. The. Fuck. I don't blush! She smiles sweetly, graciously letting my chin go so I can avoid more embarrassment. Or at least avoid seeing my embarrassment through her eyes. "You're associating the feel of this," she whips me again, and I arch my back from the pain, "with pain and humility. It doesn't have to be like that." She wraps a delicate hand around my 'cock', and I feel pleasure radiate through my body. "I want you to associate this, with this" she jerks on my cock, and flicks the whip on my nipple at the same time, sending erotic shock waves that seem to settle directly in my clit.

"Fuck!"

She leans close. "Did your pussy contract when I did that?"

"Yes, Mistress," I pant. Do it again! Do it again! I continue my silent chant until she begins stroking me gently. I'm going to come if she keeps that up. It's never been this easy for me to lose control. Is having someone control me what I've been missing? Or is it her? Her left hand continues its slow torture, while the right moves the fringed whip sensually across my tits.

My hips move of their own accord, unable to stay still with everything going on. I can't catch my breath, and it isn't long before I start feeling my world come undone. I'm pretty sure she senses the change in me, as her hand begins to move faster. Just as I feel the walls of my pussy start to contract around the dildo that's inside me, she snaps the whip on my tits, harder than any of the times before. The edge of the fringe catches my nipple, and I explode.

I yell, thrash, try to loosen my wrists, and at the same time try to close my legs to stop the seemingly never-ending spasms that are so pleasurable, they're almost painful. Now I get it. Oh fuck, I *so* get it.

The next thing I know, she's standing at the foot of the bed again, staring at me—or rather my 'cock' that's pulsing from my aftershocks—hungrily. I'm not kidding. Hungrily is a good description because she's licking her lips like she wants to devour me. Huh. I didn't know my legs could spread any further, or that I would have the strength to move even an inch. Guess I was wrong. I want more.

"In my opinion," she begins, still eyeing my 'cock', "people have it all wrong. Even those who are deeply *into* this stuff." Huh? I'm confused. Of course, my body is humming with desire, and anticipation of what's next, which is short-circuiting my brain, so confusing me is not hard to do at this point.

"This Dom/Sub lifestyle," she explains further. "Everyone assumes that the Sub is weak, and that it is the Dom that is in control."

I look pointedly at my bound hands and feet, and raise my eyebrow at her. Yeah, I can do that, too. She chuckles lightly, sending another aftershock through me. She flicks the whip directly in front of her, hitting the inside of my thighs, and right on the most sensitive part of me. It isn't pain I feel this time. This time, instead of a hiss, it's a moan of pure pleasure.

"One word, Cassidy. That's all it takes from you that could stop all of this. *You* have the power to leave me wanting. And, oh god, do I want you. If you could only feel how wet I am for you." I groan, my fingers itching to feel her, my mouth watering to taste her. "If you break the rules, you get punished, but there's always a reward for you at the end. If *I* do something you don't like, one word and it's over for me. No rewards. So, you see? *You* have the power here. *You* are allowing me to do these things to you. I wouldn't be able to do them without your permission."

Hmm. I never thought of it that way. I suspect many Doms don't. They're need for control outshines the true strength of the Sub. My Mistress is different. In so many ways, from so many things that I'm used to.

My hips have a mind of their own when she sets the whip aside, then moves her hands over her body, caressing her own breasts. She's still fully dressed, and I'm praying to anyone who will listen right now that that's about to change *real soon*. She begins to unfasten her corset, and I send thanks all around to whoever was listening.

The corset comes off, and her full breasts spill out causing my clit to throb even more than it was before. Fuck, she's beautiful. Her hands move to the zipper at the side of her white leather pants, and she finally brings her eyes to mine. Well, that is *after* I sense that she wants to tell me something, and I pry my stare off of her rosy tipped tits.

"Paying attention?" she asks with a smirk.

"Yes, Mistress." Funny. That doesn't seem so hard to say anymore. Still wish I knew her name, but we'll get there. I hope.

"You're not to move. If you move your hips, I will stop. Do you understand?"

Not really. What are you going to do to me? What if I'm unable to keep my hips from moving? It's not always a choice, you know. "Yes, Mistress."

With a slight nod, even though her look was suspicious, she continues undressing. Within seconds, this goddess is standing before me, completely nude. I think I've died and gone to heaven. This *has* to be heaven. She's shaved like I am—gotta keep up that maintenance—tanned, toned, and fucking perfect. There's a small tattoo on her hip of a bird in flight, and her belly button is pierced. So. Fucking. Sexy. I'm glad she doesn't have a six-pack. She toned, but not ripped like I am. I like my women more feminine, and she definitely fits the bill. A slight flare of her hips gives her the most perfect hourglass figure, and my body longs to be coupled with hers.

To my extreme and utter delight, she begins to crawl up on the bed until she's straddling me. Oh yeah. I feel the heat radiating from her center, and I swear it takes all of my strength to keep my hips from bucking up into her. Take me inside, baby. Please.

Starting at my cheek, her hand moves down my neck, tweaking my nipples hard, before moving down between us. She takes my 'cock' in her hand, and guides it to her opening. "Don't move," she reminds me, then sinks down onto me. She's so wet that the dildo slides in easily, and she moans in ecstasy. Of course that causes me to moan, all the while I'm still concentrating on not moving my hips.

She lifts herself, and then impales herself on me again, and I'm in awe. I watch, completely enraptured by the sensual movement of her body on top of mine. Her hips move with the grace of a dancer, caught in an erotic dance that only lovers know the steps to. Her breasts bounce in time with each thrust, and I'm about to lose it. Incredible. I'm usually a one and done kind of girl, preferring to give my partner multiples instead of the other way around. I've never had the patience to wait to get to this point.

With Mistress riding me, an orgasm seems to just be ready at any given second.

"Don't come until I tell you," she rasps, obviously noticing my change in breathing. Great. First I have to concentrate on not moving, now I have to use the rest of my will power not to come. That's impossible with the way she feels on top of me. Her hands clutch at me, fingernails digging into my stomach. Her breath hitches, and I hope she releases me soon because I'm not sure how much longer I can hold out.

She falls forward, her amazing tits swaying in my face. I wonder if she would stop if I sucked a nipple into my mouth. I decide to chance it, believing she's too far gone to stop at this point. She gasps loudly as my lips lock around a taut nipple, and I suck hard. Her left hand holds her up, while her right hand tangles in my hair, pushing me harder into her breast. I show my appreciation by biting her nipple a little harder than I normally would. She bucks wildly, slamming her body down on mine hard and fast.

"Move!" she cries. "Fuck me!"

Don't have to ask me twice! I do my best—arms and legs being tied up does not help me one bit—to give her everything she needs. My hips counter hers, and the sound of flesh slapping hard against flesh is intoxicating.

"Now! Come with me!"

Oh thank fuck! I let go with a roar that I have never heard come from my mouth before. But it's completely forgotten as I hear her cry out, squeezing my tits painfully with those last few thrusts. I feel the warmth of her come wash over me, and the sensation makes me climax again. It's the first time I've ever made a woman come like that, and if I had enough air in my lungs, I would puff my chest out in triumph and pride. But with my beautiful Dom collapsed on top of me, the most I can manage is a triumphant smile.

My *only* regret is that I am still tied up, and can't hold her as she comes down from the peak of that incredible orgasm. Well, it was incredible for me. I'm assuming it was for her, too, with the amount of liquid that erupted from her. A small sigh comes from my lover, and she weakly reaches up to release my hands. Once I'm free, I immediately wrap my arms around her, and feel her tense. Not a good sign.

She gingerly dislodges herself from me, and rolls off the bed. If my feet weren't still tied up, I would have attempted to follow her into what I'm assuming is a bathroom. I look down at my feet, contemplating the ramifications of untying myself. The game is over, right? Is it weird that that makes me sad? She walks back into the room before I even have the chance to make up my mind, and she seems surprised that I'm still tethered to the bed by my ankles.

Placing a warm washcloth on my tummy, she quietly unties the ropes, gently rubbing the redness that was left behind on my skin. I want to tell her that it doesn't hurt, but her hands feel good on me.

"I got you all messy," she says softly. Maybe it's my imagination, but I thought I heard embarrassment and uncertainty in her voice. That can't be right.

"That's quite all right. I enjoyed it immensely." I grin, hoping to show her my words are true.

Her silver eyes capture my two-toned ones. "So did I."

The way she cleans me off, gently wiping at the red marks left by the whip, brings tears to my eyes. I didn't expect the tenderness.

"Kiss me," I whisper, then silently curse when her hand stills.

"I can't."

"Against the rules?" Shit. I didn't mean to sound like that. So angry and disappointed. Especially when it caused shutters to block off every emotion in those now expressionless eyes.

"Something like that," she says evenly, turning away from me.

"So no name and no kissing. What else should I know?" Fuck! Why can't my mouth just shut the hell up? What I really want to ask her is when can I see her again. At this rate, my word vomit is going to kill any chance of that.

"Perhaps this lifestyle isn't for you, Cassidy." She kneels, and picks up my clothes. "Get dressed." She tosses them to me.

"I'm sorry." Her dressing pauses at the sound of my apology, but she says nothing. "Please, Mistress. I didn't mean to upset you." I'm still naked. I think I'll refuse to get dressed until she forgives me. No wait. Until she forgives me, and agrees to another session.

"It's okay, Cassidy. Not all of us are made for this."

"I am! With you. May I see you again?"

She's going to say no. I can see it in her eyes. Once again, my big ass mouth gets me into trouble.

"I don't think…"

"Please!" Damn. Interrupted again. Maybe it'll piss her off enough to bring me back just to punish me. "I have more to learn. I *want* to learn. With you."

Mistress finishes dressing—I'm still naked—and reaches for her mask. "Okay," she says finally, and I can breathe again. Note to self, remember to always breathe.

"When?" Shit. Eager much? I can't help it though. I've never come like that in my entire sexual life. Nor have I had multiples like that. I could get addicted to the things she does to me.

"You have an open invitation here, Cassidy. Come whenever you desire." We both smile at her play on words.

"How will I know you're here?"

"You'll know."

"It'll be you, right? I don't want anyone else, Mistress."

She nods. "It'll be me. Now, you should get dressed, and join your friends."

"I'd rather stay with you." Word vomit. Scare her off why don't ya.

She fixes the mask back over her face, hiding those amazing features. After securely tying it, she steps towards me. "You've learned enough for tonight, Cassidy. I'm sure by now Rand is finished with her 'conquest'. Celebrate with her."

"Promise you'll be here again?" Jesus! When did I get so fucking needy?

She hesitates. "Yes."

Okay, *technically* she didn't promise, but I take it anyway. I don't want to push her any more than I already have. Too risky. So I nod, and slip my shirt on.

"You're welcome to stay in here as long as you need to. There's a full bathroom through that door," she informs me, pointing to the door she came out of earlier.

"Won't someone else need the room?" And by someone else, I mean you and whoever else you pick to fuck. Thank god I didn't say that out loud. Did I? Please, please tell me I didn't.

"This is my personal room. No one is allowed in here without me. I won't be needing it anymore tonight."

Like a weight lifted off my chest, I feel like I'm actually floating. I catch her hand as she turns to leave. Bringing it up to my lips as gallantly as I can, I kiss her knuckles.

"Thank you," I whisper. Meaning it with all my heart.

She smiles softly, touching my cheek lightly before walking out of my life. Yes, I'm being melodramatic. Why couldn't we be like a stereotypical lesbian couple, and U-Haul it right then and there? Oh shit. Did I just fall for a dominatrix?

The Aftermath

RAND AND THE others were sitting in the VIP section by the time I finally gathered myself enough to leave the Pink Room. I debate whether to tell Rand about what happened. For some reason, I don't want her to know. Not because I'm embarrassed, but because it was personal. Something between me and Mistress. I don't want to share her with anyone. Not even my best friend.

"Where have you been?" Rand eyes me suspiciously.

I shrug. "Mingling. Isn't that what you told me to do?" I sit next to her, wishing I had another shot to calm my nerves. Rand sticks her face in mine and begins sniffing. "What the hell are you doing?"

"Did you have sex?"

Nosey! I *wish* I had been able to taste Mistress, but Rand isn't going to smell the scent of sex on my face. She's going to have to go lower for that.

"Did you?" I counter.

"You know I did." She actually blushes. I remember what Mistress told me, and how it was Connor with Rand without their knowledge. But it still makes me feel dirty knowing Rand thinks she was with someone else.

"And?"

She shrugs. I wonder if we get that from each other.

"It was fine."

"Just fine?" Yep. I am willing to talk about this with Rand if it means keeping her from questioning me.

"Yes, just fine. I know now that Connor is the only one I want to be with. I'm comfortable with him, and he makes me hot. That's all I need."

Shit. Mistress was right. Damn she's good. Fuck that, she's fucking amazing. Beyond amazing.

"Cass?"

I snap out of my erotic thoughts to see Rand waving a hand in front of me. Damn. She's totally going to ask more questions now.

"Hmm?" Act dumb. I can totally do that.

"What were you just thinking about?"

A smoking hot woman that just fucked my brains out, and rocked my entire world. "Nothing." Yeah. *That's* believable.

"Bullshit. Where were you? Did you hook up with someone?"

"What's with all the questions, Nancy Drew?"

"I thought you weren't 'into' this scene?"

All right, Judge Judy. I'm not liking your tone. "*You* brought me here, and told me to mingle. Now you're going to get all judgy pants on me just because I dabbled a little?" Okay, I dabbled a LOT, but I'm not about to tell Rand all that went on. Mistress is mine, and mine alone. I don't want to share her. And, yes, I realize how that sounds, and I mean it exactly that way. I'm in so much trouble.

"Dabbled?" Rand turns her entire body towards me, completely ignoring all of her other bitches, um, I mean friends. "What happened? Tell me *everything!*"

"No way! I don't expect you to tell me everything that went on with you and mystery dude!" Whoa! I *almost* let the cat out of the bag. I don't think Mistress would be happy about that. I can't believe the way I'm thinking. It's like that spectacular woman whipped the coolness right out of me. Huh. Is that where the term 'whipped' came from? Whatever. I'm still cool. Damn it. Just smitten.

Rand rolls her eyes. Damn, did she always do that, and it's just now starting to get on my nerves? "Fine. At least tell me what happened after I left. I don't need details, I'm just curious what changed your mind."

"I didn't say I changed my mind." Oh, but I did. My mind has been completely taken over by a beautiful blonde dominatrix. "Look, someone left a card on my table. It got me curious, so I asked the waitress about it." Oh, shit! What if the waitress says something about Mistress? I look around (hopefully discreetly), but I don't see her. Good.

"You got a card? Wow. I've only been here with Connor so we don't get the 'card' experience. Couples, unless it's specifically stated on the membership that they're open to threesomes or more, are not approached."

My best friend since elementary school is talking to me about threesomes as though it's the most normal thing in the world. My head may explode. It's not that we never talked about sex, but really we just skirted the issue. She enjoys hetero sex, I enjoy lesbian sex. That's enough information for me about Rand's sex life.

"But we know about the different colored rooms," she continues, oblivious to my discomfort. "I've been in all of them," she smirks, and my heart plummets. "Which one did you go in?"

"You've been in *all* of them?" That doesn't make sense. Mistress said no one uses her room except her. As far as I know, Rand and Connor aren't into threesomes. I hope.

"Mmhmm. When they're not being occupied by others, we get to use whichever room we're in the mood for. Different colors mean different things. Oh god!" she exclaims suddenly. "You weren't invited into the black room, were you?"

"What's wrong with the black room?" Curiosity temporarily overrules my heartache. I'm trying to regain my common sense over my insane jealousy. Mistress wouldn't invite a couple into her room, would she? Not if her objective was to keep couples happy with each other. No offense to Rand, she's awesome and cute, but I seriously doubt anyone could compete with Mistress.

"It's just... for advanced participants."

Hmm. I wonder if Mistress ever uses any of the other rooms. And let's just shut that thinking down right now. I can't think about that. It hurts. This can't be a normal reaction, can it?

"No, it wasn't the black room," I confess. I have a feeling Rand will freak out as much as the waitress did if I told her the color of the card I got. "I don't think I paid attention to the color. Just asked the waitress where to go."

I don't make eye contact. Rand can always tell when I'm lying, so I busy myself with looking for *her*. Is she still here? Can she see me? Is she watching me like she did before? Just in case, I sit a little taller.

"Well, what was in there? What did you do? Were you with a woman? Of course you were," she answers herself. "That was a dumb question. But the others were good, so answer them."

"No."

"Cassidy!"

I cringe. It doesn't sound as good coming from Rand as it did from Mistress. I don't want to hear it from anyone but her.

"Cass." I turn my best glare onto my best friend. "I won't ask *you* what happened in your room, you don't ask me. Deal?"

"Why are you being this way? Are you embarrassed that you might like being a Sub?"

I stare at her for a long time. "I'm not embarrassed by anything I've done, or who I've done it with. Enjoy the rest of your night, Miranda. I'm leaving." I stand before she can argue. I'm done here anyway. I doubt I'll see Mistress again, and she's all I want right now.

"Cass! I'm sorry!"

"I'll call you."

The Fall

I MADE GOOD on my promise to call Rand the next morning. That was a week ago. We both apologized, but I felt a shift in our relationship. I tried telling myself that the shift started when she announced her engagement, but I'm afraid it's been me. Something happened to me the night of her bachelorette party. The night I spent with Mistress.

I went back every night after that. I waited, drank, and waited some more. She never showed. I haven't received a shot or a pink card since. Anger started to rise inside me. She promised. Fuck technicalities! She told me she would be there, and she wasn't! And, yet, I still came back with hope that "tonight will be the night."

It's why I'm here now. Maybe I'm a glutton for punishment. Ha! Pun intended, I suppose. I'm a glutton for *her* punishment. Where the hell is she? There's no way she didn't enjoy her time with me. She couldn't have faked how she responded. How hard she came.

I signal my waitress for another drink. My third since I've been here. I should probably pace myself, but it's the only thing that makes the pain lessen. Shit. Being whipped by Mistress didn't hurt half as much as her ignoring me does. Staring into my almost empty glass, I nearly miss the card laying on my table. I look up quickly praying to see *her*. It's not. I know my Mistress's body. The woman retreating from me has a nice one, but it isn't the one I want.

I pick up the card. It's not the first one I've gotten since becoming a member here, but it's the first time I consider responding. It's black. *'It's just... for advanced participants.'* Am I intrigued enough to follow someone else? Am I *hurt* enough? *She's* not here. I'll probably never see her again. Why shouldn't I try something new? *Someone* new. My stomach turns at the thought of another woman touching me like Mistress did, and not in the good way. I flip the card around a couple of times before pushing it away. I can't.

I lay my head back on the couch, and close my eyes. My head is pounding; my heart is hurting. I need to see her. Am I obsessed with her? I really don't think that's what it is. All I know is I've never felt a fraction of the emotions and pleasure I felt when I was with her. *She* brought that out in me. I can't even imagine being with anyone else. That's going to really suck when I get it through my thick skull that Mistress is done with me.

I imagine her soft hand caressing my cheek, and I move into the ghost touch. God, it feels so real that it makes my heart ache even more. I have to get out of here. With a sigh, I open my eyes, and see the pink card laying on my table. Now, I've never been much of a runner. I've always preferred weight training. But if you saw how fast I was off of that couch and down that hall, you'd be impressed. Maybe I should sign up to do sprints. Only if *she's* waiting for me at the finish line.

I make it just as she's closing the door.

"Mistress?" My voice is unsure, and that pisses me off. Everything pisses me off. The sorrow of the week of waiting and hoping, only to be let down, comes crashing down on me when I see her silver eyes peering up at me from behind that damn mask. "Where the hell have you been?"

She closes the door with a distinct click. I don't guess she's happy with my tone. Too bad. I'm not happy either. Well, I *am* happy now that she's here, but still pissed off. Don't worry about it. It makes sense in my chaotic mind.

"Go to the foot of the bed and strip."

That's the first thing she says to me? Orders me? No explanation, no apology, just a fucking order. Fuck that.

"Where have you been?" I repeat with irritation. "You said you'd be here. You lied!"

Anger flashes in her eyes. Join the club sister. "I'm here now. And, I will not tolerate you speaking to me in this way." She won't *tolerate* it? What about what *I* had to tolerate? She continues speaking before I can open my stupid mouth again. "Say your safe word, Cassidy, and leave. Otherwise do as you are told, and go to the foot of the bed and strip."

My head falls forward in defeat. If I want to be with her—and I do—then I will have to submit to her. I guess I'm not important enough to deserve an explanation. My eyes fill with tears, so I stay facing the bed with my head down as I begin to strip. Seems appropriate that I'm wearing all black today.

"Face me," she orders. Shit. Harder to hide my tears if I have to face her. I disrobe completely—save for the dildo I'm packing—with my head bowed the entire time. "Look at me."

I watch as her eyes follow the single tear that escapes from behind my lashes. Her eyelids flutter closed, and I wonder if she's feeling even an ounce of regret for what she did to me. As she did the first time we were together, she unties her mask, lifts it away from her face and tosses it to the side. Mistress closes the distance between us, and my heartrate speeds up triple time when she reaches a gentle hand out to wipe away my tear.

"Turn towards the bed," she orders softly. She stands close enough to me that I can feel the fabric of her corset—black this time—scratch at my back. My skin burns where her hand makes contact on my left shoulder blade. In my imagination, this is her version of placing her hand over my heart. I feel the gesture deep down. "I was called out of town on business," she says quietly. "It was sudden, and I didn't have time to get word to you. I'm sorry."

Another tear makes its trek down my cheek. My breath hitches as I realize that I *am* important enough to her for her to explain her absence.

"Kneel on the edge of the bed." I guess she was getting too emotional there. Back to business. It feels wrong to even think of it that way. There's more to this than business. I know it deep down in my soul. It's with this belief that I'm able to comply with her wishes. "Hold on to the bedposts."

I glance up, noticing the ropes at the top of the posts. I'm glad my 'wingspan' is considerable, otherwise this could get uncomfortable. When I'm in position, she steps up onto the bed with help from a stepstool. It's so damn cute I almost crack a smile. The ropes are securely fastened around my wrists with only a small gasp of discomfort from me. She then dips her head towards me, and I almost faint at the prospect of her kissing me. Instead of a kiss, her warm breath caresses my ear.

"Don't fall in love with me," she whispers. Those quiet words tear my soul apart, but I manage to hold back my emotions.

She slips away from me, going to her arsenal. I'm almost hoping she gets something that delivers more pain than her words caused. She comes back with a black leather riding crop. Yes, I've been doing my homework on the items that can be used. I feel the leather move across the expanse of my back. Mistress traces one of my tattoos before moving the soft leather of the crop lower. The sting of the riding crop is intense as she slashes it across my ass.

"That's for speaking to me the way you did."

Hit me harder! I push my ass back trying to express my desire without words. Make it hurt! Make the emotional pain go away with physical pain.

"Did you get other cards while I was away, Cassidy?"

"No, Mistress," I lie.

She smacks me again in the same place, and I relish the additional pain. "Don't lie to me! Did you receive invitations?"

"Yes, Mistress," I pant.

"Did you follow through with them?" She slips the crop between my legs, caressing my wet pussy lips.

"No, Mistress." I shift my hips, trying to get the leather in a more satisfactory place. But she moves it away from me. Damn it.

"Did you want to?" The edge of the crop dips into the crack of my ass, producing a gasp from me.

"No, Mistress."

She spanks me harder than any of the times before, and I cry out. Partly in pain, partly because I want more.

"Don't lie to me, Cassidy. One more lie and this is over."

"Tonight was the first time I considered it," I confess in a hurry. "I thought you lied to me. I thought you never wanted to see me again. I thought I had done something wrong to drive you away. I waited for you every day. When you didn't show up it…" *It broke my heart. But I can't say that to you.* "I considered it, but I couldn't do it. I don't want to do this without you. I don't care about the lifestyle," *I care about you,* "if it's not with you, Mistress."

Silence fills the room. I want to see her face. I need to know if what I said affected her.

"Don't turn around!" Her voice is rougher than normal. Is she crying? As much as I want to, I don't turn around. Suddenly I hear her taking off her clothes. At least I hope that's what that sound is. As much as I love seeing her in her leather and lace, seeing her naked is *so* much better. "Stay facing forward. Understand?"

"Yes, Mistress." I barely get the 'mistress' out before my breath leaves me completely. Her warm, soft, naked breasts are pressing into my back. It's the most splendid feeling, accentuated by her erect nipples sensually poking me. I'm pretty sure I could come just from the feel of her against me like this. When her left hand comes around me to grab my 'cock' my hips jump. She begins to stroke, and I watch the seductive back and forth movement of her long fingers that are wrapped around the girth of the dildo. Each stroke slides the base of the dildo across my clit, creating the most amazing convulsions inside my pussy.

A click registers in my brain, but as it tends to happen with Mistress, my ability to think has left me. It's not until I hear a quiet whirr, and see the movement in front of me, that I understand what's going on. Somehow, with her hands quite occupied, Mistress managed to push some switch or something that reveals a mirror at the head of the bed. My eyes find hers in the reflection.

"Watch me jerk you off," she commands. God, her voice is so fucking sexy when she's horny and talking dirty. She pulls harder on the dildo to the point where she's close to pulling it out of me. I realize she knows exactly what she's doing when she roughly pushes it back inside me only to repeat the process over and over. The feel of the thick knob of the double headed dildo stretching me out moments before being thrust back into me is fucking intoxicating. My breath catches as the stirrings of my first orgasm in over a week begins deep inside.

Mistress caresses my rock hard nipple with the riding crop, never missing a stroke with the dildo. Talented. Very, very talented.

"Tell me, Cassidy. Tell me you want it."

I instinctively know she's referring to the pain of the crop. Do I want the sting of the leather across my nipple as I come? Remembering what it did for me the first time, um, hell yes!

"I want it, Mistress. Please."

Her nostrils flare, and she slams the dildo inside me, grinding my clit roughly with the base. That does it. Thank god she doesn't tell me not to come, because there's no stopping this tidal wave. I don't know how she knows the exact moment the orgasm begins, but she chooses the perfect instant to whip the crop directly on my extremely sensitive nipple.

Can you pass out from an orgasm? It's never happened to me before, but I'm convinced I lost consciousness for at least a few seconds. I'm glad for the restraints at that moment. They keep me from slumping to the floor.

"Are you okay?"

"Yes, Mistress." A little embarrassed maybe, but *totally* okay. More than okay. She gives me a small smile, patting me gently on the ass before making her way back to her treasure box. Yes, I'm perfectly aware that I called it an arsenal at the beginning of this. But if everything she keeps in there gives me pleasure that makes me pass out, it's a fucking treasure box!

I don't even watch what she selects this time. I want to be surprised. My, how things change. What once filled me with apprehension now fills me with delicious anticipation.

She climbs onto the bed again (yes, she uses the stepstool), and lays her loot down. Still not going to look. Besides, I have a much better view at the moment. Her tits. My eyes try to refuse being pulled away when she raises my head to look at her. Silly eyes. This is a much better vision.

"Can you handle more, Cassidy?"

The genuine concern in her eyes rekindles my hope that maybe this means as much to her as it does me.

"Yes, Mistress." Bring it on, baby. Give me everything you've got. I may pass out again, but I'll always be ready for more with you. She eases the dildo out of me, and I can't help but wonder what she has in store for me.

I'm mildly disappointed when she slides off the bed to stand behind me again. Then again—my body shivers with pleasure—if she keeps scratching her nail down my back like that, she's welcome to stay there forever. I feel a gentle pressure from her, and allow myself to be bent forward as far as my bound hands allowed.

That finger begins its journey again, and I gasp loudly when it finds its destination.

"Have you done this before, Cassidy?" she asks, watching my reaction in the mirror.

I shake my head. "I've never trusted anyone that much." My voice is trembling as much as my body is. This is the first time I've contemplated using my safe word with her. I don't know if I can do this.

She picks something up from the bed, but I can't bring myself to look at what it is. Suddenly I feel smooth… well… balls, for lack of a better description, being coated with the abundance of juices I've produced so far.

"Do you trust me?"

Her eyes never leave mine, and I know in that moment that I do indeed trust her. Even with this uncharted territory. I'm actually warming up to the idea of giving her something I've never given to anyone else. Sort of like giving her my virginity. I suppose technically I am a virgin *there.*

"Yes, Mistress," I whisper.

"You can tell me to stop, Cassidy. I will go slow, one bead at a time. If it hurts, or makes you uncomfortable, please let me know."

I nod, unable to find my voice as the beads slip between my cheeks.

"Relax."

Sure. Let me get right on that. I take a deep breath, willing my body—one area in particular—to relax. I feel a pressure, and automatically tense up. Her hand starts calming circular motions on my ass cheek, each time pulling them apart more and more with each pass. It's mesmerizing. The first bead slips inside my tight, um, area. Hmm. That isn't so bad. In fact, it feels pretty good. A second, slightly larger bead slips in, and I'm okay with that, too. I even find myself pressing back into Mistress, ready for more. When the third, even larger, bead slips in, I'm done.

"Enough," I groan huskily. She immediately stops.

"Do you want me to pull out, Cassidy?"

"No, Mistress." Yes, even at a moment like this I can remember the rules. "Just give me a minute, please?"

"Of course."

Her calming strokes on my ass and back never cease. I appreciate it more than I can currently voice to her. Deep breath, Cass. You got this. It's fine. We're feeling good. Filled up, a little naughty—okay, a lot naughty—and sexy. This is good.

"I'm okay."

"Are you sure?"

I catch her gaze in the mirror. "I'm sure, Mistress."

She smiles, and climbs back on the bed to kneel in front of me. "Do you remember your safe word?"

"Yes, Mistress, but I don't need it."

"Just in case, Cassidy."

She leans away for a moment, then comes back with… holy shit. She laughs lightly at my expression. The dildo looks like the one I pack, only with one big difference.

"This fits inside you, just like yours. The other parts are for me. Okay?"

I nod. She's going to let me double penetrate her. Ho-ly. Shit. I look up, and stare at that perfect ass in the mirror. That ass that captivated me from the first moment I caught a glimpse of it. She's about to give it to me. My pussy clenches, which makes other areas of me clench. Whoa. Now *there's* a sensation!

"Ready?"

My eyes snap back to her extremely amused expression. Laugh it up, baby. I'm going to enjoy fucking that ass. Immensely. I grin.

"Ready."

She slips my 'part' inside of me. Fuck, I'm so wet. I'm going to have to engage all my muscles to keep this monster inside of me. I'm up for the challenge. She leans over again. Seems like my Mistress is not finished yet. Though I'm not sure what's left. I'm certainly all filled up, and she's about to be.

There's a delicate chain wrapped around her elegant fingers. I feel suspiciously close to a sexual novice with my Mistress. No matter how much sex I've had in my past, it hasn't prepared me for all of this. But, fuck, I'm enjoying the learning process.

She cups my small breasts in her hands, pinching my nipples. The cold of the chain coupled with the pleasurable pain of her pinches make my body jerk. Jerking sends sensations all over the damn place. Good lord. I may not survive this. Ah well. I'll die happy. She squeezes a small—gulp—clamp, making it open, but hesitates before clipping it to my nipple. In a move that I was *not* expecting at all, she leans forward and takes my nipple into her mouth.

If I thought everything else she has done to me was the "best thing ever", they all dimmed compared to the feel of her hot tongue on my nipple. My hips buck, and my grip on the bedpost tightens. When she sucks, I can't hold back the groan that comes from deep inside me. She must have liked that sound because she moans, too. It sends little vibrations against my sensitive bud. Yep. I'm going to come *really* soon.

I watch her suck me into her mouth. It's the most exquisite thing I've ever seen. Or so I thought. Until her eyes came to mine, watching me as she sticks her pink tongue out, and rolls it around my nipple that I swear will spontaneously combust at any moment. She closes her teeth around me, and I shatter.

"Fuck!" I throw my head back in ecstasy, the orgasm hits me from *everywhere*. But there's no time to recover. I feel the tight pressure of the clamps on my nipples, and another spasm hits me.

"Don't move," she whispers harshly. I force my eyes open, and groan again at the site of her on all fours in front of me. That ass is backing into me as she reaches back to position the dildo. My Mistress is ready! There's no easing into anything at this point. She fills herself, pushing back with such force that it takes a considerable amount of strength to stay on the bed.

She cries out, moving faster as she brings her hand down to stroke her own clit.

Oh yeah, baby! Touch yourself!

"Oh! Cassidy!"

I bite my lip, struggling to stay still. But she's never said my name like that before. Then there's the vision of her tits swaying violently with each backward thrust, the sensation of being completely filled, and the pressure on my tits. They're all proving to be too much for me.

"Please!" I beg.

"Fuck me, Cassidy! Hard!"

I slam my hips into her ass, using my grip on the bedposts for leverage. Thank God I have strong thighs as they keep me anchored as I pound inside of her.

"I'm coming, Cassidy!"

OH FUCK! She's definitely never said *that* before!

"Me, too!" Oh! Me, too, baby! Coming with her is heaven. We cry out simultaneously, and it's fucking loud. If anyone hears us out there, good. Let them know how fucking awesome it is being me right now. I slump slightly, exhausted, but somehow needing and wanting more.

She slides me out of her, then eases the dildo out of me and tosses it to the side. She releases my nipples from the clamps, and I hiss at the flow of blood back into them, making them throb. Because there aren't enough places in me or on me that are throbbing? I feel her fingers loosening the ropes around my wrists. If it weren't for the look in her eyes right now, I might think she was done. Not even close.

"Keep your hands there until I tell you to move them. Understand?" She's panting as much as I am right now, but the authority in her voice is still loud and clear.

"Yes, Mistress."

She grabs the dildo that I wore here, and lays in front of me. Let me just tell you, when she spreads her legs, opening herself to me, it takes *everything* in me not to dive in face first. All pink and swollen. And so fucking wet. Damn, she looks delicious. My mouth actually waters, and I have to swallow constantly to make sure I don't drool. God, baby, let me down there, and give me something to swallow! If I think it hard enough, maybe she'll hear it.

It's not helping matters when she starts fucking herself with my dildo. Ever watch a gorgeous woman fuck herself for you? Spread open so wide that you feel like you're center stage for the performance of a lifetime? It's fucking unbelievable. It only serves to make me thirstier for her.

"Mmm. Fuck yourself for me."

She cries out, and her movements get faster. This time I'm not sorry that I said the words out loud. Especially getting that reaction from her. Our breathing is erratic, and my body bucks wildly with hers as though I can feel everything she's doing to herself. I'm on the verge of coming again when she suddenly pulls the dildo out of her. I whimper my disappointment until…

"Eat me, Cassidy!"

Oh, baby! I dive into that pussy as though my salvation is in there. Maybe it is. A long, deep groan reverberates throughout the room. I don't know if it was me or her, or both. Doesn't matter. She tastes as amazing as I imagined. I can't get enough. I feast on her like she's my last meal. I will be completely satisfied if she is. Believe me.

"Use your fingers, Cassidy!"

Her body writhes beneath me, and I use my left hand to keep her from detaching herself from my lips, tongue and teeth. I use my right hand to bury three fingers inside of her. I curl them slightly as I pound into her, alternating sucking and tonguing her clit.

"Cassidy!" she gasps. Her pussy walls contract around my fingers, drawing me in further.

I give up my delicious meal for a quick second to make a request. "Come for me like I know you can. Let me drink you."

Her back arches off the bed with a scream, and she gives me exactly what I want. Oh yeah! I lap her up with all the thirst of a woman who's been in the desert for days without water. That's how I felt those days without her. Now that she's with me, I'm going to nourish myself until she has nothing more to give.

The Parting

I COULD LIVE here. I make that very important conclusion as I lay exhausted, my head resting against my Mistress's thigh, her hand still fisted tight in my hair. Her breathing is still erratic. Mine? I'm taking deep breaths just to take in more of her essence. Her scent is intoxicating. Again, I say, I could live here. Forever. To put an exclamation on my decision, I kiss her mound lightly.

I sigh silently when she extracts her hand from my hair. Apparently a light kiss after what I just did to her is way too personal. Her gentle scratch on my head, though, confuses me. The signals she's sending me are as hot and cold as a Katy Perry song.

"Go into the bathroom and start the shower for us," she orders softly. A shower together? That's a plus, right? There's only one problem.

"Um, Mistress?"

She gives me a questioning look. I see what I believe is disappointment in the depths of her eyes. Oh, honey, I *want* to take a shower with you. Believe me! How do tell my Mistress that she left something, um, *behind* without looking like a complete tool. I go for the 'look back, and hope she knows what I'm talking about' approach. Her brows furrow, but I see the moment it dawns on her.

"Oh!" She wants to laugh. I know she does. She clears her throat as she scoots out from under me. "Sorry, Cassidy."

Okay, it's not funny. I have *beads* in my *ass*! She's back there snickering. Well, she's not really. I don't know if Mistress is capable of snickering. But she's patting me on the butt, telling me to relax. Relax? That was easy when I was horny as hell. Now that embarrassment has taken the place of horniness, relaxing is not really working.

"Cassidy, this is going to hurt if you don't… let go."

She even sounds embarrassed. I find it quite ironic, after everything we've done with each other, that either of us would find this situation humiliating. I take a deep, calming breath (I hope), and do my best to do as she says, and let go. With a compassionate hand, Mistress relieves me of my dilemma. It takes me a moment to stand. Not because I'm hurt, but because I don't know if I can face her.

"Are you all right?"

"Yes, Mistress." My answer is muffled because I have essentially buried my face in the bed. Perhaps if I stay here long enough I'll smother myself, and save myself from further shame.

"Come here, Cassidy."

Why do all of her demands make me feel like I'm the one who is making the decisions in this room? Without—much—hesitation, I obey, and face her. We're both still completely naked, so at least we're on the same playing field there.

"Are you sure you're okay? I'm sorry about that."

Her apology is timid. Damn, she is such an enigma. Forceful and confident one moment. Sheepish and demure the next. It makes me wonder who the real Mistress is. There's no doubt in my mind that she's a Dom. She's shown me that quite a few times. But there's so much more in there. It's enough to make me want to know everything. Her magnetism is so strong that I find myself leaning down to kiss her.

"Cassidy," she breathes, her strong yet delicate hand braces against my sternum. Damn it! Why won't she just let me kiss her? I *know* she would feel something. I sigh, not bothering to hold it in, and lower my head. "Start the shower. I'll be right in."

I know it's my imagination, but I'm going to hold on to the little hitch I thought I heard in her voice.

"Yes, Mistress."

It's wrong, and should be physically impossible, to be in a pissy mood after the orgasms I just had. And, yet, here I am. Trying not to slam doors, or throw a tantrum, just because my Mistress is driving me insane. Just as I think we could have something more personal going on, she shuts down. Maybe I'm just a damn fool. This is what she does for a fucking living. What makes me think I'm better than anyone else she's had in this room? Who am I to her but another Sub?

Great. Now I'm depressed. I turn on the shower, and calm myself before going to get her. I catch her in an unguarded moment, and my voice dies in my throat. She's standing where I left her, near the foot of the bed. She has her forehead resting against the bedpost, her hands gripping it tightly if her white knuckles are any indication. She takes two deep breaths—and, was that a sniffle? —before straightening up. Instinctively, I know she will not be happy if she knows I caught her being so vulnerable. Right before I duck back into the bathroom, I see her wipe at her cheek. If I was confused before, my head is completely screwed up now.

"It's ready, Mistress!" I call out from deep within the bathroom. I'm not willing to let her in on my little bit of voyeurism.

"Thank you."

I'm so focused on being casual, that I totally miss her entrance, and I'm startled by her close proximity. There's no sign of her earlier melancholy. I'm not entirely sure how to take that. I'll say one thing, she sure keeps me guessing.

"Yes, Mistress." I wait patiently for her next demand, wondering briefly what the fuck this woman did to me. With her, I'm someone completely different. She sweeps her hair up into a messy bun, then sways past me—with an ass like that, swaying is a requirement—grabbing my hand.

I've never showered with any of my exes. I've always considered it a personal thing. I don't want some chick watching my wash myself, or shave. I do all of that *before* I see them so I can look sexy for them. Showering with someone takes all of the mystery out of it. Or so I thought. Standing here now, seeing the water sluicing down Mistress's body renders me speechless. The mist beads on her nipples, and suddenly I'm parched. Good lord, I could drink from any part of this woman's body, and be blissfully happy.

Mistress hands me a loofah dolloped with a lavender chamomile body wash I now identify as her scent.

"Wash me."

Oh yeah. My libido overrules my confused psyche. Again, I'm ready and willing to give her anything she wants no matter what it costs me mentally or emotionally.

I bathe her tenderly, keeping my eyes locked with hers. I *needed* her to feel *something*. For me, this shower isn't about sex. It's about intimacy.

I want it to be the same for her. Maybe I'm fooling myself, but I have to try. I move closer to her, our bodies almost touching. Her breathing changes, becoming more rapid, especially when my hand progresses downward. She doesn't move. Her restraint is amazing. Even when I cup her, the only thing that gives her away is an almost inaudible moan.

Mistress closes her eyes, and I take the opportunity to dip my head. I don't dare kiss her on the lips. Yet. So I press my lips to her neck, and savor the feel of her wet, soft skin. I'm encouraged when she moans louder, and leans into me. This is good. Next stop, lips. I'm planning my route when...

"Cassidy, no." She pushes me away, but I can see how affected she is by what I'm doing. She turns away from me, rinsing off the soap suds.

"Why?" I'm taking a chance by stepping getting closer to her, but I don't care. I lay my hands on her shoulders, and she stiffens before shrugging them off. Goddamn it. I wish to hell I knew what was going on in her mind. "Mistress?" Fuck. It's times like this when knowing her name would be great.

She crouches to retrieve the sponge I had dropped in order to get my bare hands on her, and hands it to me.

"Finish in here, and then join me in the room."

Wait. What? She's getting out? Sigh. Guess so. She steps out of the shower, snapping a towel from the rod. Okay, she's pissed. Maybe she'll punish me. I let a grin form as I think about the possibilities. I don't know why I'm getting all clean when she's just going to dirty me up again. But she said to finish in here, and that's what I'm going to do. Maybe she needs a little time to set up for whatever she has in store for me. I'm getting aroused just thinking about it.

I wonder what it would be like to be with Mistress *all* the time. Am I thinking of her as a girlfriend? Hell yeah, I am. You would, too, if you felt half the things she has done to me. Would it be like this all the time? Her dominating me? Or would we make love? Mmm, making love to her sounds wonderful. What would she be like without the pain or the bondage. Both of us being in control equally. Touching, kissing...

All right, Cass. Don't get ahead of yourself. Mistress is obviously not ready for all of that. Yet. Give her a few more times with you, and *maybe* she'll be more open to the idea. I finish my shower with my little pep talk. I have a plan. Sure, right now my Mistress is a little standoffish, but all I need is a little more time.

I grab a towel from the rack. My clothes are in the room, but I'm sure I won't need them for at least another hour. More if I have anything to say about it. I dry my body—which is buzzing with anticipation—and leave the towel. I'm not going to need it anyway.

My heart plummets to my feet when I walk into the room. Mistress is sitting there as she was the first time I saw her, fully dressed. With her mask on. This is not what I was expecting, and I begin to feel sick to my stomach. If I've pissed her off enough, will she refuse to see me for a while as a punishment? Oh, god. Please don't let her do that.

"Mistress?" Yeah, my voice is wavering. I'm scared shitless.

"Get dressed and sit, Cassidy."

She doesn't look at me. I think that's what hurts the most. I'm on autopilot, obeying her demand, and before I know it, I'm dressed. But I can't bring myself to sit down.

"Please."

I sink into the chair in front of her. At this point, I don't think I have a choice. My legs feel like they may just buckle from under me.

"What's with the mask?" Of all the questions that are going on in my head, *that's* the one my mouth chooses to spew.

"This will be our last session, Cassidy."

She says it so nonchalantly that I almost can't fathom the reason my heart stops beating.

"What? Why? What did I do? If this is because I kissed your…"

"It's not that," she interrupts. Well good. I can't undo that. So whatever else it is, I can fix it. Please let me be able to fix it. "The business I was called away for? I'm opening a new club. I'll be going there to get it up and running."

"No." Eloquent. Yes, tell your Mistress no. Doms *love* that. "We—we just started. You told me you would teach me." Fuck. I'm panicking. She can't just leave me. There's no way she doesn't feel at least a fraction of what I feel with her.

"This is for the best, Cassidy."

"For who? You? Am I that bad? You can't tell me you didn't get off on all of this!" I gesture angrily towards the bed where she *definitely* got off more than once. There's no reaction from her. No flinch, nothing in her eyes change. Damn, she's good.

"It's normal for a Sub to get attached…"

"Don't! Don't fucking do that!" I stand, unable to stay seated one minute longer. I want to hit something. I want to beg her to stay. I want to go back to thirty minutes ago, and still be lying in bed with her. "I didn't get attached to my *Dom*! It's more than that. You *know* it."

She looks at me finally. "I'm sorry."

I actually believe her. But that doesn't change anything. She's still going. "Where?"

"What?"

"Where are you going? My job is flexible."

"Cassidy, you can't leave your home here."

"I'm pretty sure I can do whatever I want. Except in this fucking room." Her eyes drop, and for some reason that pisses me off even more. "Ah, I get it. It's time for you to move on, right? What's the matter, *Mistress*? Run out of conquests here? You successfully recruited me, and now you have to find more?"

I see the hurt flicker in her eyes before those fucking shutters come down in full force. Shit. Way to convince her to stay or let you go with her, Einstein. Insulting her is surely going to win her over. Then I think about her being with others like she was with me, and I can't stop the scowl. I already have a resting bitch face. Get me pissed or scared, and it becomes worse. And right now, I'm both.

"You are welcome here at this club anytime you want." Her voice is even, not betraying any emotions she may have. Maybe she doesn't. Maybe this really was just a job for her. "But this room will be closed. Indefinitely."

Indefinitely. She has no plans of ever coming back. God, how can my heart hurt this much for a woman I don't even know? Not even a fucking name, and I'm dying before she even leaves. I drop to my knees, and do the only thing I can think of. I beg.

"Please, Mistress. Please don't go. Please don't leave me."

She's on her feet the moment my knees hit the floor. "Get up, Cassidy." When I don't budge, she grabs my shoulders. "Please get up. You don't deserve this. Get off your knees." She's pulling at me almost desperately. "This world isn't for you."

"Have I not done everything you've asked of me?" I can feel the tears beginning to fall down my cheeks, and I don't care. "I may have had some issues, but I got over them. All I want is to be..." No, no, no. Don't say something to make her run even faster. "Is to be a good Sub for you."

She kneels before me, and takes my face in her hands. "God, Cassidy, you are so much more than this. I'm leaving because it's what's healthiest. For both of us." She wipes away my tears with her thumbs, but I can see her own tears forming behind the mask.

"*I should have left you alone,*" she whispers. Leaning in she gives me a feather of a kiss on my cheek before murmuring the words that will haunt me forever. "*I was selfish, and I'm sorry. I'll never forget you, Cassidy.*"

I lose track of how long I stay there, sobbing, after she walks out of my life. I can't understand how I became so attached to her so quickly. I don't know how to forget her, and move on. I'm not sure I want to.

The Return

IT'S BEEN TWO months since Mistress walked away from me. Two long, agonizing months. Even Rand is becoming concerned with my unwillingness to "join the living again". She has no clue what went on in that club. No one does. That time will always be the greatest—and worst—time in my life. And completely private. I won't invite anyone into what Mistress and I shared.

It pisses me off that I don't know her name. I can't look her up. I have no idea where she went. Hell, she could be in another fucking country for all I know. All I have are my memories, and it still hurts. I haven't been with anyone since. Believe me, I tried. But there was nothing there. No one has touched me—body or soul—the way she did. She fucking ruined me for anyone else, and *that* pisses me off, too.

Today I had decided to throw Rand a bone, and have lunch with her. It didn't turn out great. She was being too nosey, asking me about what happened in "*that club*". Yeah, it's "*that club*" now. She and Connor have stopped going. Rand even threatened to go to the management and complain that they "broke" me. It was hard not to laugh at that. If she only knew that it was the actual owner that did the breaking.

Anyway, we weren't on the greatest terms by the time lunch was over. I *may* have gotten a little bitchy, and told her to keep her big nose out of my business. Petty. Which is why I'm texting her now. Yes, it's cowardly to text instead of call, but I'm just not up for more conversation with her.

I'm sorry. Maybe one day I'll be able to explain everything to you. But for now, please just let me deal with my stuff on my own. You're married now. You don't need to worry about me anymore.

I finish typing out the last of the text, knowing that she's just going to call me later to try and get the story out of me. That's just Rand.

Fine. I'm sorry, too. I'll call you later.

See? I chuckle at the predictability of my friend. The phone is violently jostled from my hand when I bump into another person on the sidewalk. This is why you shouldn't text and walk at the same time.

"I'm so sorry! I wasn't..."

"I'm sorry..." A shocked gasp. Whether it was from me or *her* I don't know. I'm too shocked. "*Cassidy.*"

Her eyes are wide with complete surprise, which I'm sure I'm mirroring. She's back. She's *here*, in front of me!

"M—um." I can't bring myself to call her Mistress. It just seems so out of place here in front of a charming row of outdoor markets. People were bustling about all around us, but we have yet to move. "You're back." Well, way to solve the case there, Sherlock.

"Y-yes."

"How long?"

She shrugs a little, and I get the sense that she's feeling about as insecure right now as I am. Hmm. That's not the Mistress I knew. Of course, this woman in front of me is completely different than the one I met in the Pink Room. Her hair is tied back into a ponytail, her make-up is light, she has on faded boyfriend jeans, and an over-sized denim button-up shirt that is tucked into the front of her jeans. White canvas shoes complete the look, and I'm... probably drooling.

Damn. I thought she looked sexy in her leather and bustier. Obviously I only needed to see her like this to know what *real* sexy looked like on her.

"I've been back to the club a few times," I offer lamely. I'll try anything to get a conversation going with her. Now that she's back, I'm going to try anything to keep from losing her again.

She lifts a brow. "Find someone that will give you what you need?" Wait. Is that jealousy I hear? Surely I'm imagining it. Right? *She's* the one who left *me*. What does she have to be jealous about?

"No. You weren't there," I answer honestly. "I looked for you. Hoped that you would come back." I didn't say the words to make her sad, yet I think that's exactly what I did.

"I should go."

Suddenly there's only one thing I need to know before she disappears. "What is your name?"

She looks away. Oh come on! What could possibly be keeping her from telling me now?

"Did I mean *anything* to you at all?" She just stands there stock-still, unwilling to give me even one answer. My anger from the past two torturous months rears up. Never a good sign. No telling what will come out of my mouth when that happens. "You know when you told me not to fall in love with you?" Oh no. Don't say it! "There was only one problem with that, *Mistress*. You said it a little too late." Shit! I totally said it. She's shocked again, and I need to get out of there before I make an even bigger fool of myself. I march away from her. Until one timid word stops me in my tracks.

"Rebecca."

"What?" I keep my back to her, unsure if I can believe what I heard.

"My name is Rebecca."

Slowly, I face her. Rebecca. It's...

"Not what you were expecting, is it?" she asks sardonically.

"It's beautiful," I say sincerely.

"It's normal."

What's wrong with normal? Cassidy is normal.

"It suits you." And it does. The way she is right now, standing in front of me, Rebecca is perfect. Name and all.

"Not when I'm behind the mask. People assume I have some erotic name that goes with that persona. I don't."

"I'm glad you don't." I realize that it's true. I'm glad she didn't change her name to something like Mistress Payne or some such. "Why?" Oh yeah, there's the tilt of the head that I missed so damned much. Still sexy as hell. Even more vulnerable now, looking the way she looks. "Why the club? The mask?"

"That's a long story, Cassidy."

"I have all the time in the world. Rebecca." Did her breathing hitch when I said her name? I think it did. I could be just projecting how I felt saying it, but I don't care. I'll believe what I want to believe. I gesture to a bench across the way. It's nestled under some trees, so it offers a bit of shade on this warm day, as well as some privacy. "Sit with me?"

Does she always debate things in her head that should be an easy answer? I can practically see the wheels turning, perhaps trying to come up with a good excuse *not* to sit down with me. But I wait patiently— okay, semi-patiently—for her answer.

Rebecca sighs heavily, and nods. Score one for the good side! What? I'm not bad. And if I am, *she* made me that way! Whatever. We walk side by side, and my fingers itch to touch her. If I could just take her hand, or guide her with my hand at the small of her back. Is it normal to have this sense of calm and belonging with a person you barely know? One that broke your heart not long ago?

It feels like it takes us *forever* to get to the bench. I'm sure in reality it was less than a minute. But when you're anxiously awaiting to talk to someone you've been pining over for months, a minute is forever.

We settle in, and she's cuter than ever, tucking a leg up under her as she faces me.

"What do you want to know?" she asks warily.

"Everything." And it's true.

She shakes her head slightly. Probably trying to figure out how I turned the tables on her, and got her to obey me for once. I'm still trying to figure out that one myself. Going to need it in the future if I ever want to do it again. Huh. I must be confident if I think I have a future with her.

"I used to be a Sub," she begins. It's the last thing I thought I would hear coming out of her mouth. "I was just out of college. The ink was still drying on my MBA. Entrepreneurship," she volunteers before I can ask. Damn. Beautiful and smart. She intrigues me more and more. "Anyway, I had an interview for an exclusive club. They wanted someone to come in and overhaul the place. I wasn't sure I was ready for that. Hell, I didn't even know what kind of club it was, but I looked forward to the challenge. That's when I met Samantha. She owned the place.'"

She pauses. I already don't like this Samantha, and I'm not sure why. Maybe it's because my... Rebecca used to be her Sub. Nope. Don't like her one bit.

"Don't go anywhere," I plea. "I'm just going to run over to that vendor and get you something to drink. Want anything in particular?"

She gives me a small smile. "You're still as sweet as ever," she says quietly. "Water is fine, thank you."

Record time. I made it to the vendor, grabbed the waters, paid him, and was back before she had a chance to even think about bailing.

"Here you go." Fantastic. Now I'm panting. And not for the good reason.

She thanks me again, then takes a long swig from her bottle. Stalling? Maybe. Or maybe she's just thirsty. Give the girl a break.

"So. Samantha?" Yuck. Even the name tastes bitter when I say it. Yep, don't like her.

"Hmm." It wasn't a happy hmm. Or a sad one. Perhaps it was just kind of... yielding. "She was beautiful, intelligent, witty. I was instantly attracted to her."

Hate her even more.

"She decided during our interview to show me around. To let me get a feel for the club, and tell me her vision for it. When she started explaining that she wanted to turn it into a sex club, a BDSM club specifically, I didn't know whether to be intrigued, or to run as far away as I could."

Oh how I wish you had run away. But then I wouldn't have met you, so I can't be too mad. Wisely, I keep this all to myself.

"I had no idea what BDSM really was. I mean, I had an idea, probably the same one most people have, and it wasn't my thing. Kind of like you," she says with a sly smile. "When I told her that, she volunteered to 'show me the way'. I was so smitten with her that I agreed."

She stops talking again, and looks away. There's a far-off look in her eyes, and I just know she's thinking about that time in her life. Jealous, party of one, right here.

"It was the single biggest mistake of my life, trusting her," she continues, and I feel horrible for not thinking of her feelings first.

I remember our first time together, then. I had made some snide remark about letting me tie her up and hit her. She told me that she knew what it was like to get hit. Mother fucking son of a bitch! If that bitch...

"What happened?" Wow. My voice is *much* calmer than the entirety of my insides. For some reason, I have this overwhelming *need* to rip this Samantha chick's arms off, and beat her with them.

Rebecca shrugs again, and now I recognize the vulnerability for what it is.

"Samantha was never one for conventional sex. It just didn't turn her on unless she was hurting me. Or humiliating me. But it was never about *my* pleasure. There wasn't any. She would use and abuse my body until she couldn't lift the whip, or whatever else she was using, anymore. Then she would leave me tied up while she went out, and did God knows what for hours.

Even though I was tied up, I used to pray she would stay gone. But every night she would come back high or drunk, and it would start all over again."

And now I have my reasoning for needing to harm this Samantha woman. No sane judge or jury could blame me. Convict me? Sure. Blame me? No way.

"I'm so sorry, Rebecca." Lame ass words that don't take away shit for her, but they're true. I ache to reach out and hold her hand, but I'm still afraid of scaring her away.

"Don't feel sorry for me, Cassidy. I stayed with her for years because she convinced me that *that* was the way of the Sub. It was my *duty* to cater to her every whim. I was naïve and scared. But I thought she loved me. She was just teaching me her lifestyle."

"Why didn't you use your safe word?" Mist—er, Rebecca—has trained me well enough in our brief time together to know that safe words held all of the power.

"Samantha didn't believe in safe words. If you belonged to her, you had no right to tell her no or make her stop."

Jesus. This woman was living in a hell. It's a miracle to me that she's sitting here, having this conversation with me as though all of that happened to someone else. Maybe that's what helps her cope? However, as tragic as this story is, it doesn't explain why *she* now owns the same kind of club. "Where is she now?"

"Dead."

My head jerks up at the tone of her voice. It was so devoid of any emotion that I wondered—briefly—if she had done it herself.

"You're wondering if I killed her." Okay, I'm sure my eyes are about to bug out of my head. I *know* I didn't wonder that out loud. Right? "I can see the question written all over your face, Cassidy. Do you think I'm capable of that?"

"I think everyone is capable if pushed to their limit, Rebecca. But I didn't think… I mean, I just…" Yep, that's me. As eloquent as always. She smiles at me, and I melt. Shit. When the hell did I become so damned sappy? Oh yeah. Two months ago when I first met her.

"I know. The thing is, I'm not sure if I can say I didn't kill her."

Well, I certainly wasn't expecting *that* answer. But, honestly, even if she did something to cause the bitch's death, what I feel for her wouldn't change. "I don't understand."

"The official cause of death was an overdose. Samantha liked to party.

Hard. Everything she did was over the top. Drinking, drugs… me." She fidgets a little. I know this must be hard for her to talk about. The fact that she is—with me—gives me hope. Maybe it's selfish of me to think that way, but I don't intend to let this woman walk out of my life a second time.

"Did she make you?" I don't even want to finish the question. Knowing that bitch abused Rebecca is bad enough. If she turned Rebecca into a junkie, I'll find where the bitch is buried and kill her again.

"I never did drugs, Cassidy. That's the one thing I could be grateful for. Samantha was a very selfish person, especially with things that gave her pleasure. That night was no different than any other. She came home already high, and wanting more. She liked having me watch her shoot up. It made her feel powerful to let me know that I was not 'worthy enough' to participate."

Thank God for small miracles. But watching someone doing that couldn't be easy either. And then it hit me. What if Rebecca witnessed the overdose, and that's why she feels somewhat responsible? "Do you think that by watching, you killed her?"

I begin to wonder if she's going to answer. As soon as I open my mouth to tell her it's okay, she speaks.

"I felt nothing when she died. There was no remorse." Rebecca stares at her water as she swirls it around. Like a little tornado in the bottle. I'm as mesmerized by it as she is until she starts again. "Actually that's not true. I did feel one thing. Relief."

I didn't even know this Samantha woman, and *I'm* relieved she's gone. She certainly won't be able hurt Rebecca anymore. "With everything she put you through, I think that's normal."

"Is it normal to sit there and watch her take her last breath?" she asks quietly. Rebecca finally looks up at me. Though I see a myriad of emotions in her eyes, the one thing that grabs me is the strength that's there. "After she took that last hit, she became more and more agitated, which she took out on me. She kept screaming at me that I was cheating on her, that there was someone hiding in our bedroom. If she wasn't searching, she was hitting me. Then it all just stopped. Samantha raised her hand to hit me again, and just froze. Convulsions started, she began to get sick."

She shivers a little. I imagine she's back there, seeing it all over again. I almost regret starting her on this path, but I'm hoping it will help her trust me enough to let me into her life. I reach over and touch her lightly on her arm that is draped along the back of the bench. I just need her to know I'm here, no matter what. I'm glad she doesn't pull away.

"I could have called an ambulance, Cassidy. I could have called 911, and maybe she would still be alive. But I stood there, bloodied, watching her suffer, and I couldn't."

"I don't blame you, Rebecca." Somehow I know they are the words she needs to hear. Whether she believes them or not, I don't know. Jesus. How long has she been holding on to this? "She did this to herself. She doesn't deserve your guilt."

"Those are easy words to say, Cassidy."

"I know, but it's true."

She gives me a small shrug. "Fortunately for me, you weren't the only one that feels that way."

Yeah, it's irrational, but I still feel a bit of jealousy that someone else knows about this. Of course they do. She had to have called *someone* after it happened. Hey, at least I know I'm being irrational.

"You found someone you were able to trust?" I make sure to keep my voice as steady as possible.

"I don't know about trust, but he's a cop. And he knew Samantha did drugs. He always looked the other way because she gave him free access

68

to the club."

"Wait, he's a cop and he didn't protect you?" Okay, keeping my voice steady didn't last very long. What kind of bastard would just sit by while this woman was being tortured?

"He didn't know about that, Cassidy. I never said anything. Not until that night, and then it was only because there was no way for me to hide it from him. Not after what she did to me. It's why he agreed to help me, and wrote in the report that I had called him, but he was unable to resuscitate Samantha when he arrived."

I shake my head. "But that's all true from what you're telling me. She overdosed, you called him, she was already gone. Clear case."

She tilts her head at me. You know, the way I find extremely alluring? "Are you a lawyer?"

I chuckle, feeling a bit awkward doing so after such a heavy conversation. "No, but my dad is. I've listened to him discuss cases enough to know the basics."

"I see. And, what do you do?"

I know what she's doing. She's steering the conversation away from her. I could let her, but... I did mention I'm a bit selfish, right? I need to know more about her. Plus, I want to spend more time with her.

"We can discuss that later. We were talking about you."

"Aren't you tired of hearing my problems?"

She's kidding, right? "I could never be tired of you." Sigh. I peek up at her, and see the slightly surprised look. Yep, I really said that. One day my mouth is really going to get me in trouble.

"I don't know about that, Cassidy. I'm pretty boring behind the mask."

I lean closer to her. "You took the mask off for me. There was *nothing* boring about you, Rebecca. Or do you not remember our time together?"

She closes her eyes, and breathes in deeply. "I remember." When she looks at me again, her eyes are shining. It makes me want to take her in my arms, and hold her. For her benefit, I decide to change the subject back to my original curiosity.

"The club? Did she leave it to you?" I ask delicately. She snorts, and honestly, I find it very cute. I'm finding I like a lot about Rebecca just from her mannerisms alone, and I'm eager to learn more.

"No. Samantha didn't have a will. She was one of those who thought she would live forever. Truth is, when I interviewed for the job, Samantha was so far in the red that I didn't know how she kept the doors open. She was a terrible business woman. She didn't have good relationships with her vendors, she was about to lose her liquor license." Rebecca clears her throat, and takes a sip of her water. "I guess I'm not the only one she couldn't treat right."

The more I learn about this Samantha person, the more I wonder how Rebecca could have ever gotten involved with her. Just sitting here and speaking to her, I can tell she's intelligent. How did Samantha find her way in?

"I'm very good at what I do," she continues. "I graduated top of my class, and had multiple successful business plans under my belt before I even walked down the aisle to graduate. But whatever she did to that business, it was going to take a miracle to fix."

"But you did. Fix it, I mean." Obviously, since the club is still open. Thankfully. I don't think I can imagine not having met Rebecca.

"I didn't fix it for her. I bought it from her. I set up a shell corporation, and used it to purchase the club."

My Rebecca is full of surprises. Wait. Did I just call her *my* Rebecca? I'm determined to make that come true.

"Did she know it was you?"

"Not at first. I did it as a surprise for her. I was going to get it back in the black, and give it back to her. So, the 'new owner' kept her on as a manager. She kept up appearances for her staff, still acting like she was the owner." She sighs. "But losing the club sent her on a downward spiral, and things between us started getting bad. So, in hopes of making her feel better, I told her what I did. I paid for that one."

"Why, Rebecca? Why did you stay?" I'm pretty sure that's the wrong thing to ask, but you know me and my mouth. "I'm sorry…"

"Don't be," she interrupts. "It's a legitimate question. I obviously had the means." She shrugs as though she's not really sure herself why she stayed. Maybe she's not.

"You loved her." I say it like it answers everything. And, believe me, I hate saying it. I'm being irrational again, but thinking of her loving that horrible woman hurt me.

She laughs, but there's nothing joyful in the sound. "No. I hated her. At least I did at the end. If anything, I was infatuated with her at the most. Her strength and control intrigued me. She introduced me to this lifestyle, and I became addicted. It wasn't bad in the beginning, Cassidy."

"And, when it turned bad?"

"By that point, she had ingrained in my head that it was my duty as her Sub to do as she commands. Like I said before, I was so naïve and impressionable that she convinced me what she did to me was normal for those who practice this type of relationship. I hate to use that as an excuse, but I really didn't know that her version of this way of life was extreme. I know that's probably hard for you to understand."

"Not really," I confess. "I did things with you I never thought I would do without questioning it."

She frowns. "That's exactly what I wanted to avoid when I took over the club."

"I didn't mean that in a bad way, Rebecca," I explain quickly. "You're nothing like her."

"I never want to be," she says softly. "The moment she took her last breath, I stopped being a Sub. Unfortunately, that also meant I was lost. It took the staff fighting over who should take control of the club that snapped me out of it. I took over the club, fired *everyone*, exhaustively vetted a new staff, and donned the mask."

"And became Mistress?"

"Yes. Even my staff knows me only as Mistress. They don't know Rebecca. I needed my control back, and that was the start. Becoming a true Dom was the next." She glances at me as though she was debating her next words. That doesn't make me nervous *at all.* Just please don't let her tell me details of what she did with others in the Pink Room. "Every person I brought into that room was carefully selected in order to build myself up. I know that sounds callous, but I made sure that they all left feeling that everything they did in that room was their decision."

I remember feeling the same way when I was with her. Shit. I guess I really was just another notch on her whip. Talk about feeling lost. That's exactly how I feel right now.

"Is it normal for a Sub to become a Dom?" Yeah, I'm reaching for *anything* to talk about that will help me stop feeling sorry for myself. Hell, maybe I'll become a Dom myself.

"For some. Some are very set in their roles. Others use the experience as a stepping stone." She tilts her head, and her eyebrows furrow. Though I wonder what she's thinking, for the first time since meeting her I wish she wouldn't do that.

I have to start making myself understand that what we did meant nothing to her. But she said she chose her Subs carefully. How did she choose me? And why? I wonder if I would have been better off not following her that night. I quickly discard that thought, because no matter what she did or didn't feel, I had never felt more alive. Which is why I feel so bad now.

"Why me?" I just *had* to ask, didn't I? I wish so much that I didn't sound so defeated.

She lets out a sharp laugh. "Believe me, Cassidy, I tried to stay away from you." Oh great. That makes me feel so much better. I'm startled when she touches the back of my hand softly. "I didn't mean that the way it sounded. Before you walked into my club, I had decided I was done. I was getting nothing from it anymore. In fact, there hadn't been anyone in my room for months."

"A myth." I remember then what the waitress had said to me. If Rebecca hadn't been with anyone in months, it's even more confusing why she would break that with me.

"Excuse me?"

I tear my gaze away from the pattern I'm tracing on the bench. "My waitress that night. When I asked her about the card, she said she thought that it was a myth."

She nods with a little smile. "It had been a long time. But when I saw you walk in with Miranda, I wanted you."

Her words send a shiver through my body. There's a hint of desire even now, and once again I'm being confused by this woman.

"I fought with myself, telling myself to leave you alone," she continues before I can say anything. "Next thing I knew, I was buying you a drink. No matter how hard I tried to stay clear of you, my body had other ideas."

"What was so wrong with me that you tried to avoid me?" I'm hurting. My pride, my feelings. What was I lacking?

"*Nothing* is wrong with you. I tried to stay for many reasons. The biggest one being that I *knew* things would be different with you in that room." She pinches the bridge of her nose, and again, I get the feeling that she's debating just how much to tell me. "I know what you think happened with the others, but you're wrong. None of them ever saw me without my mask. None of them ever saw me naked. *You* did."

I frown. What did that mean? Were they blindfolded?

"I never had sex with any of them, Cassidy."

Wait. What? How is that possible? Isn't that what that lifestyle was all about? The pain and pleasure of sex? "But," I shake my head, trying to understand. "I… we…" Oh goody. I'm back to being eloquent.

"It was never about sex. It was about control. For both parties. That's what I meant when I said I chose them carefully. They were more interested in just giving their bodies over to the pleasure of the pain. *That's* what they got off on. I never touched them without some sort of instrument of torture. Touching me was off limits. No exceptions. Until you. I broke all of my rules with you."

"Not all of them." My head is spinning with this new information, but not so much that I don't remember how she stopped every time it started getting more personal. I may regret this question, but here I go. "Did you feel *anything* for me, Rebecca?"

"Oh, Cassidy." She scoots closer to me, and my heart triples in speed when she touches my face gently. "I felt *too* much. It's why I had to leave. It's why I should leave now." She drops her hand, and stands.

"Oh no!" I grab both of her hands, turning her until she's facing me, and hold on for dear life. "I'm not letting you walk away again, Rebecca. You said it was for the best, but didn't say why. You said it was what was healthiest, but still no reason. I *need* a reason. A *legitimate*, concrete reason."

Her expression is almost comical. She's a cross between irritated and terrified. It's the terrified part that piques my curiosity.

"I don't know how to have a real relationship, Cassidy."

I wonder if she thinks that sounds as lame as I do. It's a weak excuse at best. "I've never been in a serious relationship, either. So we'll learn. Together."

She shakes her head a little. "I'm damaged. Why would you want to get involved with that?"

"We all have our demons, Rebecca. Yours may be a bit more complicated, but I don't care. I want to be there for you."

"You don't even know me."

"I'm *trying* to! And, so far, your excuses are feeble. Give me a *real* reason!" At least she's not trying to pull her hands away. For the moment, she's *my* captive.

She blows out a frustrated breath. "Fine. You want a real reason? I am technically old enough to be your mother, Cassidy!"

"Bullshit!" Who the hell does she think she's trying to fool? If she thinks she can get away with that lie, she's sorely mistaken. And now I'm thinking about being sore… with her. Ahem. Move on, Cass. "You know I'm twenty-five, right? You can't be more than five years older than me."

"It's not nice to lie to your Mistress, Cassidy."

Your Mistress. She said it! She called herself *mine*! My nose flares with the desire I see reflected in her eyes. Get a grip, Cass! You have to convince her that you belong together before you can think of sex with her again.

"I have no reason to lie to you. The *most* you can be is ten years older than me. And that's pushing it. Besides my mom is like that much older than my dad."

Her head drops back, and she lets out this little noise. It's probably more frustration, but it still sounds sexy. When her eyes come back to mine, they're full of determination. Join the club, woman. I'm just as determined to get you to say yes to me.

"Cassidy, I'm sixteen years older than you."

"Bullshit!" Seriously, is that the only word in my 'shocked' vocabulary? Even Rebecca rolls her eyes a little at my unimaginative outburst. I can't help it! She's telling me she's forty-one years old! "Damn!"

"Exactly." Now she tries to pull away.

"Uh-uh, nope. You're not going anywhere." I spread our linked hands, and look—okay, leer—at her. "Well, shit. I just figured out what my problem has been all along. I've been dating down when I should be dating up! If this is what forty-one looks like, sign me up!"

She smiles a little, but if fades quickly. Doesn't matter. I totally saw it.

"And when we have nothing in common?" she asks.

"More to talk about." Easy answer. Come on, lady. You're going to have to do better than that. Another smile tugs at her beautiful, full lips.

"Mmhmm. And when your parents and friends disapprove?"

I'll admit to being a little worried about my parents. But not enough. "I'm an adult, Rebecca. I've been making my own decisions for a while now. Besides, like I said, mom is older than dad."

"Cassidy! I'm probably closer to *their* age than I am yours." She wrinkles her cute little nose. She's so damned adorable.

"I don't care. It's my life, and I want you in it, Rebecca." I think I'm wearing her down. So far, none of her excuses are holding up.

"Okay. How about when you're thirty-five and I'm fifty-one?" Again she crinkles her nose. I almost laugh out loud. That must be the little thing she does when she finds something particularly unpleasant. I'm guessing her age is one of those things.

"Then I hope I can keep up with you."

"You have an answer for everything, don't you?"

"When something is important to me, yes." I squeeze her hands lightly. "Rebecca, you're afraid you don't know how to have a real relationship because you've never had one. But even if you had, all relationships are different. There's no magic recipe. We work at it, and we find our own way. Nothing is a guarantee. Hell, you could wake up next week, and figure out I'm some immature idiot. It would devastate me, but at least I'll know that I was courageous enough to give it a try. I've learned enough in the times I've been with you to know that I'm willing to take a risk. I know you're scared, Rebecca. I'm scared, too. But, please, let me be the risk you take."

She stares at me for what seems to be an eternity, and I think I might spontaneously combust if she doesn't answer me soon.

"God, why can't I stay away from you?" She pulls her hands from mine, and—oh, God—wraps them around my neck. My brain is in slow motion as she lowers her lips to mine and kisses me.

The Reunion

BLISS. HEAVENLY, MAGNIFICENT bliss. That is the only way to describe the way it feels having Rebecca's lips on mine. I know I said coming with her was heaven, but I was wrong. It's being kissed by her.

"Kiss me again," I urge roughly when she pulls away. "Please, Rebecca."

She complies, brushing those luscious lips against mine. Her tongue touches my bottom lip, and I moan, opening up to her—mouth and legs. I pull her between my thighs, feeling the heat of her body against mine even through the layers of clothing. Our tongues battle for dominance, and just like its owner, my tongue submits to hers. My need for her is growing so intense, and I have apparently lost control of my hands. At the present moment, they are resting on Rebecca's perfect ass. And when I say resting, I totally mean squeezing her ass to see if I can get her even closer.

"No, don't pull away," I plead, trying to keep her in my arms. If she tells me she's not ready for this, I will die. No joke. I will keel over.

"I'm a mistress, not an exhibitionist."

God, it just does something to me when she calls herself a mistress. Maybe it's because it makes me think of everything that happened in that room. But what I want from her now has nothing to do with any of that.

I follow her gaze behind me. Sure enough, we've caught the attention of a few people. Some of the guys look like they want to join. No way, buddy. She's mine. I stand, and can't help the cocky little smile when she has to tilt her head back to keep her eyes locked with mine. If the lust behind her stare is any indication, she likes that I'm taller than her.

"Go somewhere with me," I murmur against her lips. Sue me, I needed another taste. Everyone watching can either get over it, or have fun wishing they were me right now.

"Where?" Her eyes flutter closed when I pull her even closer, and continue feathering kisses on her lips and cheeks.

"My place. Yours. Anywhere but the Pink Room." I cup her cheek in my palm. "I want to know what it's like with you outside of that room, Rebecca. I want to make love with you."

There's a bit of trepidation in her gaze, and I swear she's debating again. We're going to have to work on that.

"I don't know how," she whispers. She doesn't know how to make love? How is it possible that no one has been tender and loving with this beautiful woman? Not that I have any experience in that area, but that's been my choice. It had always just been about getting off. A bit of fun. I want so much more with Rebecca.

"Would you like to learn?" I ask, and I'm reminded of the first time we met. Rebecca—or Mistress—had asked me if I would like to learn about what they did at the club. Best thing I ever did was say yes. "We could teach each other."

"*Yes.*"

WE DECIDED TO go to my place, which is fine with me. If I get let into her world at some point, I don't care where we are. As long as we're together. I couldn't convince Rebecca to ride with me, so I watch as her sporty, silver Mercedes pulls into my driveway behind my truck.

She doesn't get out immediately, but I don't go to her. I wait for her to make the decision to join me. *Please join me.* When I see her close her eyes, and take a long, deep breath, I hold my own. *Don't leave, don't leave, don't leave.* Finally, I'm able to breathe again when she steps out. I give her a smile, and hold my hand out to her. She takes it, squeezing lightly.

Shit. Now that we're here, standing at my front door, I'm nervous as fuck. My hands are trembling, but I try to hide it as I struggle with getting the door unlocked.

"This is a beautiful home," she says. I wonder if she's trying to calm me, even though I can feel the small quiver in her own hand.

I shrug, almost letting out a cry of victory when the door finally unlocks. "It's not much…"

"Cassidy, it's beautiful," she interrupts with a bit of force. Okay. Note to self, when Mistress gives a compliment, just say thank you. I can totally do that.

"Thank you." I guide her inside, hoping to hell the place is semi-clean. I'm not necessarily a messy person, but I haven't felt up to doing much of anything except sulking. So far, so good. No dirty dishes or pizza boxes lying around. "Would you, um, like something to drink?"

"Water is good."

Water. I don't know about her, but I could definitely use something stronger than water right now.

"I have something stronger if you'd like?"

She smiles, and traces a finger across my jaw. "I want to be completely sober for this, Cassidy." She kisses me softly before stepping back again. Well, hell. I can't argue with that logic. Water it is.

"Be right back." I gesture around us. "Make yourself at home."

Where the hell is all this anxiety coming from? It's not like this is our first time together. Hell, she *tied* me up, and put things *places*, and I wasn't half as nervous then as I am now. Come on, Cass. You got this. Just do everything opposite of what you normally do. Go slow, savor her. That's easy to do. I want to worship this woman.

I nod my resolve, grab the bottles of water—eye the beer longingly—and set off to rejoin Rebecca. She's standing close to a wall with a painted mural of a beach scene. Her hand runs across the featureless face of a mermaid in the crest of a wave.

"It's not quite done." Score one for Captain Obvious. Sigh, I'm sure it's pretty clear to her that it's not done. "I—I just couldn't find my muse for the mermaid." No way I'm going to tell Rebecca that it was her face there until she left. Then it hurt too much to look at it every day.

"You did this?"

My chest puffs up a little at the awe in her voice. "Yeah." I hand her a bottle of water. "I do murals all around the city. You know, hospitals and stuff. And my friend's an interior decorator. If her clients want something a little special, she calls me." I shrug again. "Drives my parents insane, but it pays the bills, and I love it."

"You're an artist." The discovery seems to impress her. "This is amazing, Cassidy." She peers at the mural closely, as though she's trying to follow each stroke of the brush. "Freehand?"

"Yeah. I see a picture in my head, and just paint."

"Are you in galleries?"

I laugh, until I see she's not laughing. Wow. She's serious. Me? In a gallery? Nah. "I have a few canvases, but I don't think I'm gallery caliber. It's okay. I like doing the murals."

"This is definitely worthy of being displayed or sold as prints, Cassidy. I have a friend who's opening a gallery here soon. Would you like for me to talk to her?"

A friend? Or a *friend?* "Um, what kind of friend?" Shit. Totally just asked that. Damn mouth.

She smiles sadly. "You should know I don't become friends with people who have been in my room. Just one more rule I broke with you. Besides, I don't think there's a human being alive who could dominate Eve."

Now I feel like a jerk. I hope I haven't ruined things with her before they even start. Here she is, trying to help me out, and I'm worried about who her friends are. "You don't have to do that."

"I know. I want to."

I shift uncomfortably. No one has really taken my work seriously. Most think it's just a hobby. Yeah, they like it, but none of them have ever told me I belong in a place with other artists. Anyway, time to change the subject. Perhaps back to why we're here. Truth is, I'd spend all night talking to her, as long as it's not all about me.

"Okay." I take a drink of my water, assuaging my parched throat. "Would you, um, like a tour?"

Rebecca takes the bottle from my hand, and sets them both aside. "Maybe later." She pulls me to her. Oh yeah. *This* is what I'm talking about. "Right now, I just want you."

I groan. I have the urge to rip her clothes off, and just take her right here and now. But that's not how we're going to do this. I'm going to make love to her, and show her how special she is. I dip my head, taking her lips in a slow, passionate kiss. My hands get in on the act, unbuttoning her shirt, and pushing it from her shoulders. Hardened nipples strain against a dark blue, satin bra, and of course my mouth begins to water.

"You're so beautiful," I murmur as the bra joins the shirt on the floor. She says nothing, but her eyes shimmer with unshed tears. I sink to my knees in front of her, and tongue her belly ring as I unbutton her jeans. Rebecca whimpers when I take the piercing between my teeth, and tug gently. Hmm, she likes that.

My fingertips dip into the waistband of her jeans and panties. Next time, I'll be patient enough to see what she looks like in her lingerie, but right now, I need her naked. Once I have her exactly as I want her, I sit back on my heels, and just take her in. I'm almost amazed that she allows it, because I'm taking my sweet time. I trace her tattoo with a blunt nail.

"I got it after," she hesitates. I'm grateful that she doesn't want to say *her* name. That's certainly not what I want Rebecca to be thinking about now. "When I became free."

Tenderly, I kiss the tattoo, and she runs her hands through my hair. I could seriously get lost in the way she's looking at me right now. So many emotions, many I know are being reflected back to her.

The position I'm in, there's no way I can keep myself from breathing her in. My nose grazes her clit as I inhale deeply. Rebecca grips my shoulders, balancing herself. Strong fingers dig in when I use the tip of my tongue to tease her.

"I'm going to fall, Cassidy," she gasps.

I grip her perfect ass—God, I missed her ass—to steady her. "I won't let you," I purr against her glistening pussy. She's enjoying this just as

84

much as I am. I shift, the seam of my jeans giving me a cheap little thrill as it rubs against my sensitive, hard as hell clit. If I'm not careful, I could come just teasing her like this. My tongue dips further inside her, and the guttural moan that escapes me is mirrored by her. I will never forget the taste of her. I never want to lose it again.

"Baby, please."

I'm not sure what turns me on the most. Rebecca calling me baby, or her begging me. It's a toss-up. I need to have her more accessible, so I stand, grasping the back of her thighs as I do. With little effort, I lift her until she has her legs wrapped around my waist. Smoky gray eyes blaze into mine. Another note to self; my woman likes that I'm strong enough to hold her. Keep working out.

Somehow we make it up the stairs to my bedroom. It was a little precarious with our lips locked in a heated kiss. Shit. The bedroom was not a presentable as the living room. Maybe we should go back downstairs. I set her down gently.

"I'm, uh, sorry about the mess. Maid's day off." It was lame, but am I really supposed to tell her that this is where I spent most of my time when she was gone. If I slept, I got to dream about her. "But, um, the sheets are clean. I just changed them."

Her brows furrow. "Not sure I want to think about why at this point."

Oh shit! She thinks someone else has been in here. "No! I just mean it was time. Rebecca, I haven't been with anyone since… well, since I met you." There. I told her. It's the truth. Even when I tried to be with others after she left, I couldn't even get to the deep kissing point. It always felt like I was cheating on Mistress. I don't regret my decision, even if she has had others in her "room".

"Neither have I. Even before, Cassidy."

Relief washes over me, but because I'm me, I still have to hear it. "No one wherever you went? You know, breaking in the new club?" Damn it. Couldn't just quit while I was ahead, could I?

"No." She sighs, and I wrap my arms around her in an attempt to apologize. But she continues before I can say anything. "I didn't lie to you when I said I was leaving for business. But it wasn't for another club like the one here. I was consulting on a business venture. I just wasn't able to concentrate."

"Why?"

"I couldn't stop thinking about you." I get the feeling that Rebecca keeps telling me things that surprise even her. I hope it's always like that with us. Lord knows I rarely have a filter, especially when it comes to her. I basically told her I loved her, for fuck's sake.

"Is that why you came back?" Please say yes!

"Cassidy, I'm feeling very vulnerable here." She looks pointedly at her naked body, then my fully clothed body. My clothes are off in seconds, and she's chuckling. I grab her, and pull her to me, reveling in the feel of her body touching mine. "You're not wearing it."

She's used to seeing me packing, but I haven't felt the urge to put it on since she left. Besides, I didn't need it with the way I was feeling, and I told her as much.

"I missed you," I continue. Opening up to her so she knows it's safe to do the same with me. "I didn't want to do anything but sleep. At least then, I could dream about you. I had no idea where to find you, or if you were even still in the country. I didn't even know your name. But I missed you so much that I was dying inside."

Her eyes shimmer with tears. My own tears fall unchecked, until she reaches up, and captures them with the pads of her thumbs. "I missed you, too. It felt so wrong in my head to want you, but my heart ached. I couldn't stand being so far away from you anymore. I didn't think I'd ever see you again, but I needed to be closer to you. You were here,

I needed to be here, too."

"Rebecca." I rest my forehead against hers, and let the emotions engulf us. I've stopped questioning how I can feel this much for someone I barely know. Some things in life are just meant to be. That's how I feel about Rebecca. It was just meant to be. I was in that club, at that moment, for a reason. And she's standing right in front of me.

"Make love to me, Cassidy," she breathes.

"Do you want me to get…"

She silences me with her fingertips. "No. I want to feel you."

Mmm, I want that, too. I guide her to the bed, nudging her back gently as I kiss her. We don't break contact even as I crawl up there with her. I begin to lower myself on top of her, and something changes. Rebecca's hands are on my chest, *pushing* me away. After everything we just said to each other, this can't be happening.

"What's wrong?"

"I'm sorry. I…"

There's fear in her eyes. Fear? What could she possibly be afraid of? I would never hurt… shit. I never even gave thought to whether she would have intimacy issues after everything she'd been through. The other times we had been together, *she* was in control. I was never on top of her.

"Does this scare you?" I ask gently.

She nods, and averts her eyes.

I hold myself up, making sure not to I'm not trapping her in any way. "Oh, baby, you have nothing to be ashamed of. We can try this another way, it's okay. I just need you to know I would never hurt you. Never, Rebecca." I reiterate with passion.

When I move to switch our positions, she stops me.

"Wait, please? I want to feel you on top me."

"I never want to do anything that makes you uncomfortable. We can try this another time."

"I'm okay. I want this, baby. I just panicked for a minute." She wraps her arms around my neck, effectively stopping me from going anywhere. "I'll tell you if it's too much. I promise."

I take a moment to think of the best solution, but she's pulling me down on her. If this is what she wants, I'll comply. I'm determined to make her forget everything except what's going on between us right here, right now. We both moan at the contact of our bodies. The feel of her beneath me is intoxicating. The sound of her accelerated breathing, her soft whimpers as I kiss her neck, her louder sounds of ecstasy as I take her nipple in my mouth, and move my body on hers, are riveting. All I want to do is keep doing things that cause those sounds. I know I've said this before, but it's heaven!

Rebecca's body writhes under me. Her hips lift, pushing her wet, hot center against my thigh. Then she lifts her knee, and I nearly explode at the feel of her smooth, strong thigh against my clit. I'm soaked, and the sound of us together fills the room with an undeniable erotic charge.

"Touch me, Cassidy," she breathes close to my ear, causing tremors throughout my highly aroused body.

Oh yeah. I slip a hand between us, getting my first feel of her in more than two months. "Mmm, you feel so good."

I didn't realize I had said the words out loud until her fingers clamped onto my ass, squeezing and pulling at the same time. Encouraged, I slip two fingers inside her, remembering how she had enjoyed when I curled them, and hitting a particularly sensitive spot.

"I need to touch you."

Her plea hits me straight in the clit. She's *finally* going to touch me. No way I'm passing up this opportunity! I shift slightly, staying inside her while I get to my knees. She scrapes her fingernails—a different shade of pink today—down my ribs, then dips her fingers between the lips of my sex. Rebecca's moan is hoarse and needy when she feels how wet I am for her. I don't think I've ever been this wet before. I know what horny feels like, this is *so* much more than that. This is unmitigated need.

"I've wanted to do this since I saw you walk into my club," Rebecca confesses before slipping two fingers inside me.

"Oh god!" My hip buck involuntarily, drawing her deeper inside me. *This* is heaven. Yeah, I know I'm using that word a lot when it comes to her. It just seems like the closer I get to Rebecca, the better it feels. Each thing I feel or learn tops the last. I want nothing more than to keep learning. Keep feeling. Her.

I pump my hand faster; my curled fingers are being sucked in even more with each thrust. Rebecca matches my drive, and as if by some unspoken agreement, we each slip another finger inside. At this moment, I'm glad I don't live in an apartment or have roommates, as neither of us have it in us to be quiet. Rebecca grips my hair with her free hand, our hips pump passionately in unison. I'm so close, but I'll hang on for as long as I have to in order to come with her.

"Cassidy!"

Oh fuck, yes! "Rebecca!" Don't ask me how I manage to get *anything* coherent out. But the need for her to know that I'm right there with her—*Rebecca*, not Mistress—was too great.

The rough sound that comes from deep within Rebecca is what sends me over the edge with her. She pulls my hair as she comes around my fingers, and the intensity of the orgasm that rips through me has me seeing stars. Jesus fuck, I have *never*—even in the Pink Room—felt like that before!

"It was you."

Panting, Rebecca looks up at me. "What?"

"It wasn't what we did in that room. It's *you* who makes me feel this way, Rebecca."

If I could have predicted what saying those words to her would do, I would have chanted them over and over like a mantra. Her pussy contracts—even more—around my fingers that are still buried in her, and she cries out. I feel the warmth of her orgasm trickle between my fingers. Um, yeah. There's no stopping this domino effect. Hell, this can go on all night, and I'll be a happy camper. Completely depleted of any kind of bodily fluid, but fucking happy about it.

"You're the only one that's ever made me do that."

This revelation of hers nearly sends me over the edge *again*. I can't help but feel pride in that accomplishment. I give her a cocky grin, and she laughs softly. My grin turns into a whimper as she pulls her fingers from me. Thinking she may need a little break, I do the same. But it's not a break Rebecca needs. She plunges her fingers—still soaked from me— inside herself. Fuck. Me. That is the sexiest thing I've ever seen. My woman isn't done yet, though. Fingers now coated with both of our juices are promptly reintroduced to my greedy pussy.

I groan, rotating my hips, thinking of how her come is now in me. This has to be the most sensuous thing that has ever been done to me. And remembering what we did in the Pink Room, that's saying quite a bit. Then she does something that blows my mind. She brings her coated fingers up to her mouth, and licks, tasting *both* of us. She hums her approval, and I want a taste. I *need* a taste. I dip my head, sucking her fingers into my mouth. I did mention before that I was greedy, right? I lick those fingers clean, savoring each and every drop.

I collapse beside her, happier than I've ever been. "That was incredible," I gasp out.

Rebecca rolls on top of me, smiling. "Yes, it was." She gives me a quick peck. "How's your stamina? Because I'm not even close to being done."

"Oh, I can do this *all* night long, baby." I hope. Fuck the age difference, it's going to be *me* struggling to keep up with Rebecca. But, oh, I am *so* up for the challenge.

"Good to hear. Why don't you get your little friend?"

Oh yeah! It's just getting started!

The Promise

I'VE NEVER BEEN one to snuggle. Yeah, I've slept with a couple of my exes, but once the sex was done so was I. However, waking up with Rebecca wrapped around me—naked—is… well, heaven. Come on, you had to expect that.

She's using my chest as a pillow. I think that's what woke me up. Her warm breath is tickling my nipple, making it hard. Her leg is draped over my thighs, and her delicate hand is resting over my heart. It's a wonder she can't feel it beating out of my chest.

I've been awake for a while now. Just listening to her breathe makes me dream of a future with her. We talked a lot last night. Yes, talked. We needed breaks, so in between orgasms, we learned more about each other.

Last names, likes and dislikes. The more I found out about Rebecca, the more I needed to know. Does she want children? Or maybe we could start with a dog. Wait, what if she's a cat person? Why wasn't this something I asked about last night? I lose all train of thought when I feel a hot tongue rolling across my nipple.

Rebecca hums as she takes my taut bud into her mouth. The vibration of that hum, coupled with the feel of her sucking, good lord. Unfortunately, she ends her little assault with a distinct little pop, looking up at me with a smile.

"Good morning."

"The best." I return her smile, pushing her tousled hair out of her face. "How did you sleep?"

"Like a baby. You?"

"Never better," I answer honestly, kissing her gently on the forehead.

Rebecca's rolls my nipple between her fingers, sending electrical currents down south. "How long have you been awake?"

"Um." Shit. I'm not going to tell her I've been sitting here wondering if she's a cat person, and what we're going to name our pets, whatever they may be. "Not long." I hiss when she pinches my nipple. Hard.

"Mmhmm. Try again."

I let out a short laugh. "About fifteen minutes or so." Give or take five or ten minutes.

"What were you thinking about?" The gentle stroking she's giving me doesn't match the mischievous twinkle in her eye.

"Um." Okay, I really need to get better at my 'on the fly' answers. "Can I ask you a question?" That's it. Turn it back onto her. Now I wonder if I'm going to have the courage to actually ask the question that popped into my head.

She chuckles as though she knows exactly what I just did. "You didn't learn enough last night?"

See? I told you we talked! "I could never learn enough," I answer seriously. "The more I discover, the more I need to know, Rebecca." A faint blush graces her features, and I find it delightful.

She clears her throat, fidgeting a little. "What's your question, Cassidy?"

Oh crap. Okay. I can do this. "Do you…" Is it hot in here? "Do you…"

Rebecca leans back, apparently extremely amused at my inability to articulate my question.

"You're cute when you're flustered."

I raise my eyebrow. "I am not flustered." There. I sound rightfully miffed. Then she pinches my nipple again, and I laugh. "What are you? A lie detector test?"

"Yes. You'd be wise to remember that," she teases with a cute smirk. "Now, what's your question?"

You got this, Cass. Just ask. "Do you…" Shit.

"I got that part," she laughs. "Try different words."

Damn it. Just say it. I take a deep breath. "Do you think you could fall in love with me?" Whew. I hope she got all of that, because I said it so fast even I had a problem keeping up with myself. I peek down at her, and find her smiling brightly. That's a good sign, right?

"Yes."

She said yes. My heart does a little jump for joy, and I know I'm grinning like a fool.

"Do you think you've already started falling?" Fuck. I couldn't have just been happy with what I already learned, could I? No. My damn mouth had to keep on going. The breath I'm holding releases as soon as her hand caresses my cheek.

"Yes," she whispers.

In a flash, I reverse our positions, and pin her beneath me. "You know, we *are* lesbians."

Rebecca laughs. "Really? What tipped you off?"

"Cute. What I mean is, we should take advantage of this stereotype we have. We've had three dates, that means a U-Haul is totally acceptable."

I'm probably pushing it. In fact, the flash of anxiety in her eyes tells me I am. I can't help it. She left me once. How do I know she won't get scared again?

"We have *not* had three dates."

Okay, not what I expect, but something I can work with. At least it wasn't an outright 'you're crazy'.

"Sure we have. The first two times at the club, and now. Or last night. If we make love right now, that'll be four. Which if you need four dates, I'm totally willing to sacrifice," I grin.

She laughs, and shakes her head. "Sex? Sex is what constitutes a date for you?" Well, yeah. I shrug. "There was no food involved."

"Food? That's a date for you? Food?"

This is one thing different about our ages so far. Girls that I've gone 'out' with, are really only interested in one thing. Sex. They couldn't care less if we went out beforehand. Maybe it's not an age thing. Maybe it's just a difference in what is really wanted out of the relationship.

"For starters, yes," she laughs. Rebecca wants food? That's what she'll get. I move to get up, and she catches me by the ass cheek. "Where are you going?"

"To see what I have in the fridge. I'm going to make you breakfast, lunch, and dinner." I frown. "I think maybe I have some eggs. I know I have some beer."

"Such a bachelor," she mumbles playfully.

"Not anymore," I vow, making a mental note to stock the house with foods and items Rebecca wants. I try to get up again, but she stops me.

"Cassidy. Don't rush this."

Damn.

"I'm not trying to, Rebecca. It's just…"

"You're afraid I'll run again," she states, filling in the blank I left. I shrug again. That's me. Master communicator. "And I'm afraid you'll find someone younger, and more beautiful."

"Never." There is no one more beautiful in my eyes. And her age doesn't matter.

"I could say the same thing to you. I'll never leave again. I told you we would try this, and we will." My long bangs fall over my worried eyes, and she tucks them behind my ear. "But we're going to have to prove it to each other. If we're going to trust each other together, we're going to have to trust each other when we're apart."

Oddly enough, that makes perfect sense to me. Not that I like it. It wasn't just fear that prompted me to bring up the U-Haul stereotype. I loved waking up to her. I want to keep doing that.

I give an exaggerated, resigned sigh. "I know. But you'll still stay here sometimes, right?" A lot of times, I amend silently. If she won't move in, maybe I can at least get her to stay more often than not.

"Of course. We're in our honeymoon stage," she waggles her eyebrows at me, and I chuckle. She's so damn cute. "We'll be together more than we're apart, Cassidy. We just need to know we *can* be apart without *falling* apart."

It sounds like she's trying to convince herself as much as she is me. I decide to give her a break, and I agree. "No problem. We totally got this." I kiss her soundly, eliciting a soft moan from her.

"Totally," she murmurs against my lips before deepening the kiss.

My stomach, traitor that it is, chooses that moment to complain loudly that it needs food. Obviously that causes Rebecca to break the kiss out of laughter.

"Hungry?"

"I missed dinner last night," I pout pathetically.

"Aww, poor baby." She pats my ass, giving it a little squeeze for good measure. "Up. Let's get some food inside you."

"I'd rather have *you* inside me." Stupid stomach decides to roar its complaint again, and I fight not to blush when Rebecca snickers.

"You'll have me. But you need some sustenance. I think your stamina needs a bit of a boost."

I'm tempted to show her just how good my stamina still is. But she's right. If I want to keep on going like the Energizer bunny, we're *both* going to need fuel.

"Fine. Can you cook?" Me? I'm a lousy cook. Unless it's toast. I make a mean toast. Except when I forget about it, and it comes out the consistency of charcoal.

"I have many talents," she answers saucily with a wink. No doubt. "However, I think even my abilities won't be enough for possibly expired eggs and beer."

I grin sheepishly. She probably right about the eggs. I don't even remember when I got them. I flop over to my back as she scoots out from under me, propping myself up on my elbows. "Want me to go pick something up?"

"No." Rebecca bends over—oh yeah—to pick up my shirt. I think she just realized that hers is downstairs somewhere. "I know of this great little diner not too far from here. Plus, it's close to the gallery I was telling you about." She pads over to the bathroom door. "It can be our first date," she winks.

I love the sound of that. I find myself *wanting* to go out with her, and show her off to the world. *Maybe* people will have a problem with our age difference. *Maybe* mom and dad will not approve. But looking at her right now, dwarfed in my shirt, hair disheveled from all of our activities the night before, nothing or no one can tell me that she's not right for me.

"Rebecca?"

She pauses at the bathroom door, a small smile playing at her lips. "Yes?"

"Will you still teach me?" As awe-inspiring as making love with Rebecca was last night, I still want what she gave me in that room. I'm not sure how to explain how free I felt, even with being tied up. My inhibitions left me, and I turned my body over to a beautiful woman whom I trust never to hurt me. At least not more than I'm physically able to handle. She has the potential to hurt me emotionally like no other. But, as Rebecca said, we're going to have to prove to each other that we're here to stay.

Her eyebrows shoot up towards her hairline. "You still want to do that?"

"Yes. Only with you."

The only indication that what I said affected Rebecca is the fact that her nostrils flare with desire.

"Lay down and spread your legs, Cassidy."

Oh yeah. I smirk. "Yes, Mistress."

Guess who was the appetizer that morning. It took us a little while to get out of bed. And the shower. And bed, again. Which of course led to another shower. Trust that when Rebecca says she has many skills she's not lying one bit.

The Mistress

REBECCA

I SIP MY tea as the melodic sound of making a Skype call fills the air. I just left Cassidy, promising her that I would meet her again for dinner. We *finally* made it to Ellie's Diner after quite a long 'session'. Turns out, Cassidy is a very quick study, and makes an excellent Sub. I almost felt guilty this morning, doing what I was doing to her. But she assured me that it was what she wanted. We'll have to set up some ground rules if we're going to keep up this part of the relationship. I'll do anything not to turn out like Samantha. Not that I think I will. I would never hurt Cassidy intentionally. Better safe than sorry.

My thoughts are interrupted when the call is accepted, and a friendly face fills the screen. Another session of a different kind for me today.

"Good morning, Rebecca."

I smile. "Good afternoon, Dr. Woodrow." Dr. Willamena Woodrow, psychiatrist extraordinaire. After what happened with Samantha, I needed more help than I imagined, and I found it here. How we do things is a little unconventional, but it works for us.

She returns my smile, and I find it comforting and familiar. "The offer is still open for me finding a colleague in your area. They would be just as qualified to work with you."

I shake my head. She offers this to me every session, and I turn her down each time. "I like this setup. Besides, you come highly recommended."

"Very well," she laughs. "How are you feeling today?"

I can feel my mouth split into a bright, all out smile. "I'm feeling great."

"Well! I don't think I've ever seen you smile like that. What—or should I say who—is the cause?"

Oh boy. We've already had the Cassidy discussion, and she knows my concerns. She allowed me to talk then without interjecting with her ideas. I wonder if she'll do that now.

"Cassidy."

Her eyebrows raise. "The young woman you've been telling me about?"

I roll my eyes. Of course she had to throw 'young' in there. "Yes."

"I thought you weren't going to see her again."

It wasn't a judgmental statement. I *did* say that. Still, it rubs me the wrong way and I scowl. "It wasn't planned. I ran into her on the streets. Literally." I take another sip of my tea, trying to rein in my emotions. "We spoke, and I decided to give us a try."

"What made you change your mind? You were pretty adamant about not dating Cassidy because she was too…"

"Young?" I finish for her. "She changed my mind. She's a fascinating woman. Intelligent, beautiful, funny."

"Rebecca, you don't have to convince me of her attributes."

"She told me she loves me," I blurt out. I didn't think I would divulge that so quickly, but it has been on my mind since Cassidy said it. Okay, technically, she didn't *say* it right out. But the implication was there. Loud and clear.

"And how did that make you feel?"

I come close to snorting tea out of my nose. "You are such a shrink!"

"That's what it says on my degree," she winks. "Seriously, Becca, did it scare you when she said it?"

The nickname makes me feel safe and cared for. "Sure it did, Aunt Wills. But mostly because I think I feel the same thing for her."

"This is awfully sudden. Not that I don't believe it can happen this quickly. It did with your parents. I just hope you're ready for what's to come."

"Being judged?" Aunt Wills nods. "I've been judged most of my life. Being gay usually puts a pretty big target on your back. But Cassidy seems confident that it won't be a big issue."

"And, what about you? The gap is pretty significant, Becca. You had legitimate concerns about that."

"I did. *Do.*" I answer truthfully, choosing to ignore the 'significant' gap comment. "But we talked quite a bit last night," as well as doing many, many other things. "We found that we have a lot more in common than we expected."

"Last night? So this is a very recent development?" I nod. "I would advise you to take it slow, Becca."

"We discussed that. She already asked me to move in, but I think she was half joking."

"What did you say when she asked that?" Aunt Wills now sounds a little skeptical of my girlfriend. Girlfriend. What a heady word for me.

"I know she's scared that I'll run again, and that's what prompted her to ask. But I told her not to rush things. That we needed to trust each other apart in order to be together." Or something like that.

"That's level ten psychiatry there, Becca," she teases. "So, I take it you're going to wait to sleep with her? Again, I should say." Yes, my aunt knows about my sex life. She's not much older than me, even less years than there are between Cassidy and me. That makes it easier for me to be open with her. She's always been more like my big sister.

I avert my eyes. "Well, um, no. We made love last night."

"As Rebecca or Mistress?" Mmhmm. She knows I'm a mistress. That one is still a little uncomfortable for me—and for her.

"As me, Aunt Wills." She nods, and writes something in her leather notebook.

"And how did that make you feel?"

"*Shrink*," I mumble. "Safe. Loved. Amazing. I never knew it could be like that." Another note. "You think I'm making a mistake, don't you?"

"Absolutely not." Aunt Wills sighs, dropping the shrink persona. Believe me, I know the difference. I do it, too, when I switch from being Rebecca to Mistress and vice versa. "This is why they tell you never to treat your family members. You're too invested emotionally. I promised my sister that I would look after you, Becca. I failed…"

"Stop right there, Aunt Wills. You didn't fail at anything."

"I should have seen it. I'm a psychiatrist for heaven's sake. I should have known what Samantha was doing to you."

"I hid it well. You can't blame yourself for any of that."

"Does Cassidy know?"

"She knows everything," I divulge. "And, she didn't take off running. She said she didn't blame me."

Aunt Wills nods. "I'm going to ask you one question as your

psychiatrist. And, then, I'll give you my opinion as your aunt, someone who loves you."

"Okay."

"Do you think your feelings have anything to do with the fact that she is the complete opposite of Samantha, and holds you blameless?"

If I didn't know that Aunt Wills also thinks I did nothing wrong, I might be offended. But she's playing devil's advocate. "I don't think so. What I feel for Cassidy has nothing to do with Samantha, and *everything* to do with how Cassidy makes me *feel*."

"Very good." Aunt Wills sits back in her comfy, leather chair, dropping the shrink persona again. "I love you, Rebecca. You are my niece, my sister's daughter. All I want for you is to be happy. Judging from the smile you had when I asked how you were, Cassidy accomplishes that. It doesn't matter to me what the age difference is. You're both adults, and there's absolutely nothing wrong with you two being together."

Tears sting the back of my eyes, but I will them to stay put. "Thank you."

She gives me a warm smile, and I can see why she's such a successful psychiatrist.

"When do I get to meet her?"

Oh lord. "Um." Heh. Cassidy is already beginning to rub off on me. Mmm. Rubbing on Cassidy. Focus! "As my aunt or my shrink?"

"Either. Or both. If you feel she would benefit from talking to me…"

"Let's just keep it simple for now. I'll tell her about you, who and what you are to me, and then she can make her own decisions."

"Sounds reasonable."

"I *can* be reasonable," I laugh, and check the time. "Oh, look at that. My hour is up."

"I suppose you want the family discount again?"

"Of course. Thank you for talking with me today, Aunt Wills."

"Any day, any time, Becca. You know that. Are you meeting Cassidy soon?"

"Yes, for dinner. Our second date," I grin. We say our goodbyes, and log off. I glance around my apartment. Not a bad place, but after spending the night and morning with Cassidy, I'm actually feeling kind of lonely. *Not* a reason to be renting a U-Haul, but definitely a reason to get ready a little early. Perhaps Cassidy and I can have a bit of an appetizer. My grin widens. Hmm. Having Cassidy as a girlfriend is going to be fun.

The End

Acknowledgments

This novella started out as a dare. It was actually meant to be just a quick short story that I would *maybe* share on my website (hence the tongue-in-cheek title). It turned out to be one of my favorite stories I've written. I love Rebecca and Cassidy (Cass if you're not Rebecca). So much so that I've connected this book to my others. Rebecca and Cass return in the next LA Lovers novel.

With all of that said, my first thank you must go to Josie. Who knew that a weird conversation would lead to this? I not only thank you for the idea/dare, but for being a beta reader, and giving me input on the cover design.

Karen, it's always fun having you as a beta reader. I love that you can see the characters as real people like I do. You and Josie helped me create a book that took me out of my comfort zone, and I can't thank you enough for that. I'm happy with the results. ☺

Writing sex scenes is by far the most difficult part of writing for me. This book—being erotica—was just one ball of difficulty. It's a delicate balance trying to put into words the passion, as well as a vulnerability, that will make the reader connect to the characters. I hope that I have accomplished that.

Of course, I'm always grateful for those who support me no matter what I write. I know this subject—whether it be the BDSM lifestyle or the lesbian lifestyle—is not for everyone. My goal is never to offend anyone. But I also don't want to limit myself because of what others may think. So, to those of you who believe in the whole of my work, I thank you.

Daisy—I'll have to learn new ways of saying thank you for being in my corner. ☺ My genre of writing may not be your cup of tea, but that never stops you from supporting me. Maybe one day I'll put pictures in my books. ;)

All the Sunday Ladies—I hope you all enjoy this one. ☺ Thank you all for your continued support. #TRFL

Angela McLaurin (Fictional Formats) —Beautiful work from a beautiful person. You know you'll always be my go to!

Jim McLaurin—I can't thank you enough for being open-minded enough to read this, and fix my mistakes!

And, my message to my readers—I know there are people who race through books like they're the breath of life. To some, they are. I write for the same reason. I need to. I can only hope that my writing allows you an escape from the stress life can sometimes be. I would like you to always want to say "just one more chapter." ☺ Peace, love, and light!

About the Author

I've been in Houston, Texas, writing novels and designing websites since 2009. Moving here was one of the best decisions I've ever made, because I've been able to live wonderfully, and write my heart out. I've always enjoyed the arts in one form or another. Music sets the mood, reading stimulates my brain, and writing allows me to utilize my imagination in any way I want. I've been writing stories since I was a teen, and figured out writing was my passion when I finished my first novel, Something About Eve.

I love being captivated by books that lead me into different, exotic places, and through impossible scenarios. I love being able to become someone else for a time. Reading has always inspired me to bring my own characters out to play. My hope is that *my* writing will inspire others, or at the least, give them a way to escape from everyday life for a little while.

As web designer, etc. for singer/actress Deborah Gibson, I've had the opportunity to be involved in wonderful experiences, travel around the country and meet exciting people. I was able to travel back to Berlin, to meet more fantastic people. It's experiences like this, I believe, that help me create unique, and (hopefully) lovable characters.

I will be continuing the LA Lovers series with Ellie's (from Ellie's Diner) book next. Each book will be a stand-alone, but look for Rebecca and Cass, as well as others, to pop up. I truly hope you enjoyed Mistress (Rebecca) and Cassidy as much as I enjoyed writing for them. Thank you for reading!

Where You Can Find Cameo Characters & Places

Eve Sumptor-Riley

Something About Eve

Flawed Perfection

Coming Home

Dr. Willamena Woodrow

Eve's Blogs

Ellie's Diner

Coming Home

Flawed Perfection

Connect with Jourdyn Kelly

My Website (http://www.jourdynkelly.com/)

Twitter: (https://twitter.com/JourdynK)

Goodreads (goodreads.com/author/show/2980644.Jourdyn_Kelly)

Facebook (https://www.facebook.com/AuthorJourdynKelly)

Instagram (https://www.instagram.com/jourdynk/)

Amazon Author's Page (http://www.amazon.com/-/e/B005O24HK8)

Printed in Great Britain
by Amazon

34773669R00070